# HIS RELUCTANT COWBOY

A.D. ELLIS

"Need a ride?" the man with a full day's dark scruffy face topped with a black cowboy hat leaned out of the truck window as he brought the vehicle to a stop on the side of the narrow, dusty, back country road.

Though the man was handsome enough to stop traffic, Reid Alexander scowled and shifted his designer travel bag to his right shoulder. "Don't you know it's dangerous to pick up hitchhikers?"

"Are you a hitchhiker?" Cowboy smiled. "From the looks of your clothes, you're a city boy through-and-through. Never been outside the city limits. Those fancy boots would do a lot more good on a catwalk than this old country road. Bet you've got some damn painful blisters if you've walked over a mile." The man cocked his head. "And from the looks of you, you've been walking for a while."

"No, I'm not a hitchhiker." Reid's shoulders drooped. "That obvious, huh?"

"Well," Cowboy drawled, "if the boots and bag didn't give you away, the red jeans, cat sunglasses, and no hat are a neon sign over your head flashing *City Slicker* in rainbow letters."

"Fine," Reid huffed and propped a fist on his hip. "I'm not a hitchhiker, and I'm not from around here. But it's still not safe to talk to strangers."

Cowboy's green eyes twinkled. "And yet here we are."

Reid narrowed his eyes and pursed his lips before glancing at the wide-open area of nothingness around him. "And just where *are* we?" His feet hurt, his stomach was grumbling, and the sunscreen he'd applied too late wasn't doing much to cool the fiery skin on his neck.

The man laughed. "Where were you supposed to be?"

Reid frowned. "Well, I'm trying to find the damn Pine Ridge Ranch. But, after driving for three days, my car decided to shit out on me. I was in the middle of BFE with no cell service. So I started walking."

The cowboy quirked an eyebrow. "I'm impressed. How long you been walking?"

Reid shrugged. "I walked about an hour and came

across this dinky little store. Not even a gas station. But the guy had water and some snacks. Luckily, I had some cash because he definitely wasn't accepting credit cards. He said the ranch was about two miles down the road. Probably should have asked to use the phone, but I wasn't sure who to call. Plus, I just need to get to the ranch. So I bought some sunscreen, a couple extra bottles of water, and snacks and started walking." Reid glanced around again. "But I think I've been walking more than two miles." He sighed.

"Well, you're in luck." The cowboy smiled. "You're not far from the ranch, and I'm heading that way myself. Hop in."

Reid frowned. "Says every serial killer at the beginning of their murderous rampage." He shifted his bag and began walking. "No thanks." He tossed the words over his shoulder as easily as he tossed his golden, light brown locks from his forehead.

The truck moved forward, keeping pace with Reid's steps.

"Seriously, I'm heading straight to the ranch. It's only about a half mile, you didn't veer off course too far." The man held out a phone to Reid. "See? This is us." He pointed at the little dots on the digital map. "And there's the ranch."

"How do you have cell service out here?" Reid yanked his own phone from his pocket and glared at the screen.

"Not very many services reach way out here. The one I've got is about the only one." He tossed the phone onto the seat next to him. "But I can't use that phone anywhere but out here. It's totally useless."

"How do I know you're not just trying to lure me into your truck so you can kill me and spread my body parts all over the vastness of South Dakota?" Reid dropped his bag and stood with both hands on his hips.

The man chuckled. "Well, now. I guess you won't surely know that until I deliver you in one piece to the ranch. But, honestly, I've got a shit ton of work to do, so if you don't want the ride, I'll just be on my way." He pointed out the window. "Take that little side road up there. Follow the dust from my tires if you need. And put on some more sunscreen. Your neck looks like it could blister any moment." He started to pull the truck away.

"Wait!" Reid grabbed his bag. "I feel like I'm going to die whether it's from the heat and walking or from you taking way too much pleasure in killing me. So I'll take the ride. I'm dead either way."

Cowboy stopped the truck again and laughed. "Dramatic." He shook his head. "Throw your bag in the back and climb in."

Reid did as he directed and then slid into the front passenger seat. "Thanks. Oh my God, it feels so good to sit down."

"Sorry, this is my work truck. It doesn't have air, but

with the windows down the breeze should feel pretty good now that you're out of the sun." Cowboy pulled the truck back onto the dusty road.

"No worries." Reid's head lolled on the headrest for a few moments before he turned toward the driver and cracked open an eye. "What's your name?"

"I could tell you, but then I'd have to kill you." Cowboy quipped.

Reid sat upright. But instead of grabbing for the door handle, he started ranting. "Listen, I'm having a damn shitty day. Actually, a damn shitty week. Month. Maybe even a damn shitty year. I'm tired. I'm hungry. I'm completely out of my element. And I'm doing a really huge thing by trusting you enough to get me to the damn ranch. Is it that hard to tell me your name?"

Cowboy's eyes grew wide. "Walker. My name is Walker."

Reid slumped against the truck seat. "Thank you. Nice to meet you. My name is Reid Alexander."

Walker nodded. "So, Reid Alexander, what brings you to *BFE* South Dakota?"

"It's a terribly long, terribly shitty, terribly ridiculous story that I really don't have the emotional fortitude to get into right now." Reid kept his eyes closed and his head reclined on the seat. "Suffice it to say, I'm here to do what needs to be done so I can get the fuck out of this wasteland."

Walker was quiet for a nanosecond. "Sounds like a

man with a plan. Hope it works out for everyone involved."

"Honestly, I don't really care if it works out for anyone but myself," Reid snapped. "I don't have the time for this. And I don't want to be here. But it's not like anyone asked *me* what I wanted."

"Well, I don't know what it is you need to take care of at the ranch," Walker started, "but I do know a handful of families have worked and lived there for generations and would be lost without it. Maybe something to think about."

Reid glared at Walker. "Thanks for the input. I'll keep it in mind." Reid rolled his eyes.

Walker made a left turn onto a smaller path and drove about five hundred feet until a large gate brought the truck to a stop. Walker keyed in a code and the gate slid open.

"A ranch that has a gated entry?" Reid knew his words held too much bite. "Better make sure the cows don't get stolen."

Walker shook his head. "You know much about the Pine Ridge Ranch?"

"Enough to know I have no plans on staying any longer than necessary."

"Figured as much." Walker nodded. "Pine Ridge doesn't run many cattle; definitely not enough to keep the ranch running. Horses are the bread and butter here."

"Horses?" he squeaked. "Of course it has to be horses."

"Got a problem with horses?" Walker frowned.

"Not my favorite animal." Reid shrugged. "I thought ranches were for like a thousand cows to roam and eat grass."

"Some are. But Pine Ridge isn't big enough in mileage or fertile enough in grass for cattle to graze." Walker pulled the truck to a stop in front of a large farmhouse. Several other farm buildings stood around the area. "This ranch breeds and trains the best horses in a two hundred mile radius. Well-known for rehabilitating horses, too."

Reid climbed from the truck and immediately scrunched up his nose.

"Sorry, City Boy, guess you're not used to such earthy, natural smells, huh?" Walker laughed.

"If by earthy and natural you mean *shit*, then no, I'm not." Reid tried to take a breath and nearly gagged. Putting his arm in front of his nose, he reached for his bag.

"Chicken wingin' it ain't gonna work forever, ya know?" Walker slapped Reid on the back. "Come on, I'll show you to the office."

"If that's where the person in charge can be found, lead the way." Reid frowned from behind his arm. "And I won't be here *forever* so it doesn't matter."

Walker led Reid to a building that looked somewhat

like an excessively large garage. Several people, looking very much like modern day cowboys, talked and moved around in all manner of work. Some walked horses, some rode horses, some carried large bags on their shoulders, some hefted bales of hay from the back of a large wagon.

"So, this is like really a ranch?" Reid muttered into his arm.

"Really a ranch?" Walker laughed. "Yeah, it's *really* a ranch. Like I said, known for the best horses for over a hundred miles." Walker opened a plain aluminum door at the corner of the barn. "Come on, office is in the main horse barn."

"Oh, fuck no." Reid stopped dead in his tracks. "I'm not going near horses."

"Relax. The horses are housed here, but they won't be near you. We're just going to the office. Most of the horses are out of the barn right now anyway." Walker gestured for Reid to walk through the door.

Reid entered the building and squinted while his eyes adjusted to the lack of sunlight.

"You can take your arm away. Your nose is likely used to the scent by now." Walker shook his head and veered to the right and down a hall. "Here's the office." He pushed open the door and let Reid enter first.

Reid rolled his eyes. "My nose will *never* get used to that stench." But he removed his arm and shrugged. "It's just not as strong in here." He sat in one of the chairs opposite the large antique desk in the middle of the room.

"Same hay, manure, feed, and horse smells are in here as much as out there, but you tell yourself whatever makes you feel better." Walker smiled. "I'll let the foreman know you're here." He turned to leave.

"Wait," Reid cried. "I mean, I didn't get to say thanks. For the ride I mean. And, you know, for not murdering me. I appreciate it."

Walker laughed, throwing his head back to reveal a long, muscular neck and prominent Adam's apple. "I like you, kid. You're funny." He walked forward and shook Reid's hand. "You're welcome. The ride and not killing you were my pleasure."

Reid blushed and shook Walker's outstretched hand. "Maybe when I'm ready to leave this damn place you can give me a ride? Back to my...well, shit. I'll need to get my car towed and fixed before I can leave."

Walker held Reid's hand and stared at the younger man. "The ranch will see to it that you have a way to get back home." He released Reid's hand and turned again to leave, but paused at the door before speaking. "My grandma used to tell me, 'Don't let fear keep you from trying something new. You may find out you love it.'"

Reid scowled. "Okay? What's that got to do with me?"

Walker shrugged. "Just thinking out loud. Different

doesn't have to mean bad. Different can be new and good."

"Whatever you say, man." Reid continued to scowl. "Can you just let the head honcho know I'm here?"

Walker gave a nod and closed the door behind him.

## 2

*T*he door opened and closed behind Reid. He shifted in his seat just as the man who had entered spoke.

"Good day, Mr. Alexander." He held out a hand to shake. "I'm Walker Corrigan, the foreman of Pine Ridge Ranch. What can I do for you today?"

Reid shot from his chair. "Are you fucking kidding me? You damn sneaky ass piece of shit. You think you can play me just because I'm not from around here? Pull one over on the gay kid because he's got no clue about a South Dakota ranch? Been laughing at me since you picked me up, huh?" Reid kicked the wall, but winced when his blistered feet screamed in agony. "Did you tell all your cowboys about the city slicker? Get them laughing at me?"

Walker watched Reid's tirade, with both arms

crossed over his chest. When the younger man seemed to run out of words, chest heaving, red faced, waiting, Walker spoke. "Are you done?"

"I don't want to be. I'm pissed. But I'm tired and need to sit down. So, yes, I'm done." Reid flopped back down on the chair. "For now."

"I have almost no idea why you're here," Walker began.

"Close to no idea?" Reid narrowed his eyes.

"Well, I know the esteemed owner of this ranch was an Alexander. God rest his soul. I know he passed away, much to the extreme sorrow of all of his ranch employees." Walker walked to the opposite side of the desk and sat down. "So, I'm guessing you're here because of Mr. Alexander's death. He was your grandfather, right?"

"Yeah." Reid frowned. "How did you know that?"

"He used to talk about his grandson all the time. But he called you a different name, and the pictures he'd show us were of a younger kid." Walker smiled slightly. "I'm sorry for your loss."

"No need. I didn't even know the man," Reid snapped.

"Why did he call you Jackson if your name is Reid?"

Reid rolled his eyes. "I'm named after my father and his father and his father. But I hated that name almost as much as I hate my father. So I use my middle name. It's more fitting." He picked at a hangnail on his thumb. "I don't know how he got pictures of me."

Walker shrugged. "Someone had to be sending him the pictures. He used to get them every six months or so." Walker paused. "I've been here fifteen years. The pictures stopped about four years ago, maybe?"

Reid was silent for a moment. "Must have been my mom. She was always trying to convince my father to contact my grandfather. She probably sent the pics."

"You were probably about ten years old in the first pictures he showed us. But the sender included some baby photos, as well." Walker reached down and opened a small refrigerator. "Water?"

Reid nodded and caught the icy bottle that was tossed his way. "Makes sense. My dad refused to speak of his father or family for a long time. I think Mom did some digging and found out names and addresses. Pissed my dad off royally." Reid laughed. "I bet he found out about the pictures and put a stop to her sending them."

They sat quietly for several moments while the daily sounds of a horse ranch filled the air around them.

"So, Reid Alexander, what brings you to the Pine Ridge?" Walker twisted his lips into a wry smile and waited for what he assumed was going to be bad news about the ranch.

Reid hesitated, chewing on his lip. "Well, like I said in the truck, it's a long, shitty story. Suffice it to say I'll be here for a bit of time. Any chance I could get a shower and some food and we could have this discussion when I'm not bone tired?"

Walker raised his brows. "A bit of time? We talking days? Weeks? Months?" He held up a hand. "Don't get me wrong, you're welcome here at any time for as long as you'd like. I'm just intrigued as to the reason for your visit."

"I've got the story and the paperwork to explain everything." Reid sighed. "But I really don't feel like I can do it justice just yet."

"Understandable." Walker nodded. "Total transparency here, Mr. Alexander. I recall what you said about doing what you need to do and not caring if anyone gets hurt." He paused.

The two men locked gazes.

"I'd like you to take a good hard look around this ranch and realize that the workers here are people with families. Look at the people you'd be hurting with whatever it is you think you have to do. Whatever it is, I'd beg you to let me help you think of another way." Walker hoped the younger man would take his words to heart.

Reid closed his eyes and pinched the bridge of his nose.

"Well then, follow me." Walker stood and made his way toward the door. "I'll get you set up in the main house and have Cook make you something to eat. A shower, some food, and a nap and you'll be good as new."

Reid nodded and followed Walker from the office. He kept his gaze straight ahead and refused to look at the horses or the workers. He'd come for one reason and one reason only. The sooner business was taken care of, the sooner he could head back to California and whatever life held for him there.

"Oh my God." Five tiny dust mops on legs scuttled toward Reid, barking and jumping. He dropped to his knees in the main entryway of the house and allowed the dogs to climb all over him, licking, yipping, and wiggling. "Hello, hello, aren't you the most precious little puppies?"

A throat cleared behind him. "Those were your grandfather's dogs. He had four mama dogs during my time here. Usually sold off all but a few of the litters. For some reason, this last litter, he kept all the pups. Their mama was killed by a coyote about a year ago, so these five are pretty much spoiled rotten by the entire ranch."

"So they aren't really puppies? Just small?" The five dogs continued to clamor over Reid.

"Nah, they're Affenpinschers, a small breed. About two years old. But they love people." Walker grinned at the dogs using Reid as their jungle gym. "Usually don't get this excited over strangers though."

Reid laughed. "What can I say? I'm special."

"'Course, most visitors don't drop to their knees so easily either."

"It's a talent," Reid purred and winked up at Walker.

Walker cleared his throat again. "Yeah, well. Let's figure out where you're going to sleep. I'll have our ranch cook, Norma, make you a sandwich, at least."

"Listen," Reid stood from the floor still holding one of the dogs while the rest begged at his feet. "I don't mean to put anyone out. I don't need any special treatment or anything fancy." Reid pointed out the window. "I can even stay in one of the bunkhouses or whatever they are called. I just need a mattress and a shower."

"Nothing doin', no way your grandpa would allow his grandson to sleep in a bunkhouse." Walker moved past Reid and waved him forward. "Come on."

The dogs followed too, and Reid laughed as he put the fifth dog down to join the crew. "It's like a little parade."

"They think they're going to get a snack or something. Usually once they sniff the visitor they go right back to their naps." Walker's gaze followed the small herd of dogs scuttling across the expansive hardwood floor. "Norma, this is Reid Alexander."

The older woman, who could be described as stout and fluffy, gasped and rushed around the kitchen island to pull Reid into a hardy hug. "Oh, Mr. Alexander. Your grandfather was so very proud. I've waited for the day you would come to us."

Reid blushed and stammered, "Ah, well, thanks. It's nice to meet you." He slowly removed himself from her clutches.

"Can you set Reid up with something to eat, please?" Walker asked. "I'll show him to a room and let him shower. He'll probably eat and then nap."

"Thank you, Ma'am." Reid nodded toward Norma.

"Oh, I know just the dinner we shall have to celebrate tonight," Norma exclaimed as she busied herself banging pots and pans. "A meal fit for one such as you, Reid Alexander. I must get busy. Go, go now, rest." She shooed him from the room.

Walker led the way from the kitchen, and Reid and the dogs followed.

"She doesn't need to cook a special dinner," Reid hissed as they moved from Norma's earshot.

"No need to argue." Walker waved a hand. "She'll cook whatever she wants, whenever she wants."

Reid shrugged.

"Okay, so you have the option of your grandfather's old room, or any of the three guest rooms in this wing of the house." Walker gestured to four doorways. "Or, you can pick from three rooms in the other wing. That's where my room is."

"One of these is fine." Reid pointed to the doors. "But I don't want his room. That's weird."

Walker chuckled. "He would have loved having you here." He walked to one of the doors. "This one is probably the best room. It's a replica of the one your grandfather assigned to me when I moved into the house."

"Why?" Reid asked.

"Why what?" Walker frowned.

"Why give me the best room, and why did he move you into the best room?" Reid's tone sounded somewhat accusatory.

Walker was quiet for a brief moment. "I think he was lonely. Your grandmother died long before I started working here at the ranch. Your grandpa had a longtime girlfriend when I came here, but she passed away when I'd been here about five years." Walker opened the door to the bedroom and walked in. He continued speaking as he opened the curtains and looked out the window. "The previous foreman and his son lived in the main house at one time."

"What happened to them? Why aren't they still living here?" Reid threw his bag on the bed and slipped off his boots.

Walker started to speak, but had to stop and clear his throat. "Accident. Foreman's son was driving them home from an auction one night. Drunk driver hit them head on, killed them both. Drunk walked away with barely a scratch. I think he served fourteen months or something. Such a damn shame, lost two incredible men."

"I'm sorry, that sucks." Reid joined him by the window. "When was that?"

"Almost four years ago." Walker turned from the window. "Jack promoted me to foreman and moved me into the main house. It was good for both of us. Kept each other company. He and Greg had been as close as brothers. Losing Greg and Samuel was hard on him."

"So, it's just you and Norma in here now?"

"Yeah, huge house, plenty of space. Which is why there's no reason not to take the best room with the best view." Walker gestured out the window. "Look at that. That's Pine Ridge Ranch. Your grandfather's dream, his pride and joy, his legacy."

Reid's eyes stung, but he blinked away the burn and pursed his lips. "It's beautiful. But his dream isn't my dream." He sighed. *Don't let the charms of this man and the ranch sway you, Alexander.* "I'm going to shower if that's okay," Reid abruptly changed the subject.

"Yeah, that's fine." Walker moved to the adjoining bathroom. "You've got your own bathroom in here. Towels, toiletries, everything should be stocked. Laundry gets picked up three times a week and returned the next day. Laundry room is in the basement if you need to wash something on your own. But I wouldn't recommend it. The crew that does the laundry is pretty specific about their routine. Probably best not to butt in." Walker gave a little wave as he crossed to the doorway. "I'll be out in the office until late afternoon. After dinner, I'll be in the office here in the house. Come find me when you're ready to tell me what the devil brought you here."

Reid nodded. "Hold up," he called abruptly.

Walker turned.

"So, I'm sure it's fairly obvious that I'm gay." Reid set his jaw in a show of defiant challenge.

Walker said nothing, simply raised his brow.

Reid huffed. "Is that going to be a problem?"

"For who?' Walker cocked his head.

"Me? You? Others?" Reid flicked both hands in the air in a gesture of frustration. "Do I need to be worried about the employees or families taking an instant dislike to me because of my sexuality?"

Walker snorted. "Depending on why you're here, your sexuality will be the last thing they hate you for." He turned and walked from the room.

$\mathcal{W}$ alker entered the kitchen where Norma was busy whipping up a feast.

"Oh, don't look like someone kicked your puppy," Norma teased. "This is a good thing." She nodded and patted Walker's shoulder.

"I don't know." Walker leaned against the counter and shook his head. "Part of me knows Jack wouldn't ever do something to put the ranch at risk." He pinched the bridge of his nose. "But Reid had no emotional attachment to his grandfather and has no reason to appreciate this ranch. I don't know for sure why he's here, but I've got a feeling it's not going to end well."

Norma tsked. "Nonsense. Jack Alexander was the best man I knew aside from my dear Benjamin, God rest his soul." She held a hand to heart. "If Jack had a reason for wanting Reid here, we have to trust it. The man was unconventional in a lot of aspects of his life, but he almost always got the job done *and* done right."

"*Almost always* is the part that worries me." Walker shoved away from the counter. "I'll be in the barn until dinner. Send him my way if he's looking for me."

"You hush. We have to stay positive. This ranch has been part of many families' lives for a very long time. It will not just wither and die, blowing away with the dust." Norma shooed Walker away. "Go on with you. I have dinner to prepare. The way to a man's heart is through his stomach."

"Not that you aren't a catch, but I'm pretty sure he's not interested." Walker chuckled as he thought back to his recent conversation with Reid.

"You're not interested either, but you'd do just about anything I asked of you for a plate full of enchiladas or a slice of chocolate cake." Norma wagged a finger and smiled knowingly.

"Point taken." Walker raised his hands in defeat and left the kitchen.

REID SHUFFLED INTO THE KITCHEN, his hair still wet from the shower.

When Norma turned, she beamed before frowning. "Dinner will be special. You'll need to dress better." She eyed his gray capri sweats and "Boys Wear Pink" tank.

Reid narrowed his eyes for a moment. "You throwing shade at my sense of fashion?"

"Attitude is neither wanted nor appreciated in this house." Norma scolded. "I have no issue with your fashion. I happen to think men can wear any color they want, and you look quite nice in pink. I'm simply letting you know that I won't bust my fanny to cook the best damn food you've ever eaten only to have you show up to the table in ratty sweatpants." She planted both hands on her hips, obviously waiting for his reply.

"Pretty sure you just became my very favorite person on this ranch." Reid winked.

Norma laughed. "And you've not even tasted my cooking."

"Can I help with anything?" Reid eyed the large kitchen with the many food stage preparation going on.

"No, but you can put your butt in that chair and eat this sandwich." Norma took a plate from the fridge and uncovered a monstrous sandwich, a pickle spear, and potato chips.

"That's the biggest snack I've ever seen." Reid's eyes widened as she placed the plate before him. "No way I'll be able to eat it all, but thank you, it looks delicious."

Norma went back to her work as Reid dug into his food.

"Where did you come from?" Norma asked as she checked pots on the stove.

"California," Reid said around a bite of sandwich. "North of Los Angeles."

"You like it there?"

Reid shrugged and stuffed a chip in his mouth. "My parents live in a ritzy, flashy area, so it suits me fine."

Norma hummed in answer. "What do you do there?"

"I don't have to work, thanks to Daddy dearest. So, I spend most of my time taking dance lessons and volunteering as a dance teacher at a youth center." Reid chomped on the pickle spear.

"That's a beautiful thing." Norma nodded. "I'd like to see you dance someday. My husband and I used to dance. He was a talented dancer. Me? Two left feet. But he was patient and never let me sit on the sidelines."

"Maybe I can teach you some moves." Reid winked. "Did he work at the ranch? Your husband?"

"Mmm hmm, my dear Benjamin. He was a horse trainer." Norma smiled. "I've lived on this ranch since the day we married. Benny had started as a stable boy about the time Jack was taking over the ranch from his elderly father, your great grandfather, Jack."

"Another reason I go by my middle name. Too damn confusing with all the Jack's."

"Anyway, Jack quickly saw Benny's skill with the horses and promoted him." Norma stirred a simmering pot. "We were married a month later. Lived in the bunkhouses and I helped the old cook. Grumpy ass old man, he was, but a damn good cook. Taught me at least half of what I know."

Reid finished the last of his sandwich and smiled as he propped his chin on his hand to listen to the tale.

"When Cookie passed on, Jack moved me to main cook. Benjamin and I moved into the main house, opposite wing from Jack." Norma's gaze turned wistful. "He'd been courtin' Sarah for over a year while working his butt off trying to keep the ranch up and running."

"I thought the ranch was the best around?" Reid frowned.

"It is now. Wasn't always the case. Great grandpa Jack took it over from his father and kept it afloat, but was never really able to make it meet its potential." Norma shook her head. "Wasn't until Grandpa Jack took it over that it really started to thrive. That man died at age ninety-seven, and at least seventy of those years were spent devoted to the Pine Ridge." Norma walked over to the table. "Thought you'd never be able to finish the whole thing." She smiled.

Reid blushed. "Hungrier than I thought, I guess." He brushed crumbs into his hand and stood to throw them away. "So you were here when my father was born?"

Norma's face scrunched up. "Yes, I was. Can't say I ever took a liking to *that* Jack. Think we were all relieved when he demanded to be sent off to school. Maybe letting him go away so young wasn't the best move a parent could make, but young Jack seemed determined to make everyone around here miserable if *he* was going to be stuck living a miserable life on a *ranch*. From the time that kid was born, he seemed to look down on anything he deemed *beneath* him, and that included ranching."

Reid nodded. "Yep, sounds about right. Did he ever come back after leaving for school?"

"No. Never saw him again. I didn't ask, but I got the feeling your grandfather only heard from him when he needed more money. Benny told me that your father had been promoted through school and entered college early. Graduated, with honors, early, as well. Became a huge success in the business world." Norma frowned. "Good for him, I guess. I think it always hurt your Grandpa Jack that his son was so unlike himself. Sarah was a beautiful and wonderful woman, but she wasn't a very motherly type so they never had more children."

"What did Sarah do here at the ranch?"

"She was mostly in charge of event and entertainment. She also made sure all of the children were looked after and educated." Norma cocked her head to the side. "Funny that she was a better mother to the ranch children than to her own. Sad, really. But maybe because the ranch children loved and appreciated her, I'm not sure Jack Junior ever really did."

"He still doesn't." Reid shook his head. "I think my mother only stays with him because it allows her to volunteer and support non-profits. And maybe because of me." Reid smiled, but it was a sad smile as he thought about his unfortunate relationship with his father. "I think she knows Dad would likely toss me out if she wasn't there to run interference." Reid batted his lashes. "I know it's hard to imagine, but I can be a bit of a handful."

"Why would your dad throw you out?" Norma was fishing, and they both knew it.

"He, ah, doesn't exactly *agree with my lifestyle*," Reid deepened his voice as he mocked his father.

Norma snorted. "As if who you are is something you can choose."

Reid beamed and slapped a hand on the old wooden table. "Right?"

"I mean, if we could choose who we are, wouldn't most of us choose to be rich or famous or thin? Personally, I'd like to be rich enough to never need to work and still be able to help others, and eat whatever I want without getting fat. Oh! And be able to sing." Norma shook her head. "Why would anyone *choose* to be something that may bring them a lifetime of ridicule and harassment? People's thought process on that never makes sense to me."

"Exactly." Reid pressed his lips together before taking a sip of sweet tea that had magically appeared in his hand at some point in the conversation. "I love who I am, and I wouldn't change it, but it's taken me a fairly long time to come to terms with the fact that I don't match the perfect, idealized, cookie cutter image that society has for what a man should be. I'll never have the perfect wife, white picket fence, two point five kids, and a dog."

"As well you shouldn't," Norma stated. "You should have whatever makes *you* happy and makes *you* feel complete. Husband? Kids? Dog? Sure, if that's what fills your heart. Boyfriend? No kids? Cat? Maybe. Just a great group of friends? The kids at the youth center? A parakeet? Whatever makes *you* happy."

Reid finished his tea. "Great group of friends probably isn't in the cards."

Norma wrinkled her nose. "You don't have a huge group of wildly artsy, eclectic friends?"

"Sorry to burst the stereotype." Reid winked. "Nah, I've never really built strong, long-lasting friendships, or relationships. Everyone around me seems so superficial, only in it for themselves or for what my family's money can provide." He wrinkled his nose. "That's why I stick to dance and the youth center. I can be alone and happy in dance, and spend time with truly appreciative people at the youth center. No one there knows I come from money."

"So, forgive me for prying, but humor an old lady, there's no special someone waiting for you back home?" Norma wagged her brows.

Reid snorted. "Not in the least. In fact," he yawned

before continuing, "my most recent *boyfriend* suddenly stopped calling when he realized I wasn't an instant heir to my grandfather's fortune."

Norma grunted. "Well, good riddance to him." She threw her arms around Reid's shoulders. "Your Grandpa Jack was so very proud of you even though he never got to meet you. You've come to a wonderful place, you're welcome here for as long as need be, and you'll never be without friends."

Reid gave a small smile. "Don't go makin' things harder than they already are."

Norma arched a brow.

He simply shook his head. "Never mind. I just don't want to get too attached. I won't be staying long."

"My boy, I think it's already too late. I'm feeling all sorts of love for you. Plus, you've got to teach me to dance." Norma hugged him close to her side. "You may find ranch living is just what's been missing in your life."

*L*ater that evening, after eating the best meal Reid of his entire life, and that included the most upscale restaurants on the west coast, he insisted on helping Norma clean up the kitchen. Walker checked on the horses, and most of the other ranch hands who had accepted the dinner invite went to finish their chores.

Several of the children and their mothers stayed at the main house. The dog crew loved having the kids to play with, and the mothers laughed with each other and Norma as they packed up leftovers and washed dishes.

"Whoa, whoa, whoa," Reid stood, hands on hips, at the kitchen entry. "What's wrong with this picture?"

When all the women gave him a blank look, he continued. "Ladies, this is not the 1800's where the little missus is barefoot and pregnant, making sure the hardy stew is ready for the menfolk. Why are only females in here cleaning up?"

Norma laughed. "Well, dear boy, I happen to get paid a nice salary to cook and clean up. I'll let the others defend themselves."

A beautiful young woman with olive skin, deep brown eyes, and ringlets of dark hair rubbed her belly. "Personally, I'd much rather be in here. It's cooler, smells better, the company is great, and I don't have to worry about stepping in horse poop." She pointed behind Reid. "My brother adds to the male population."

Reid had learned at dinner that the young woman was Shay. She was married to a young, black ranch hand named Wes. They had a little girl, Elise, and a baby expected within five months. Shay's brother, Ezekiel, lived with them on the ranch.

"What about the rest of you?" Reid frowned at the other women.

They shrugged and one of them spoke up. "Same as Shay. I enjoy the company. I love horses, but I don't want to muck stalls. It's not a male/female thing. I just would rather talk with my friends, watch the kids play, cuddle some dogs, and not get stinky."

Norma's eyes twinkled. "Why are *you* in here?"

Reid pursed his lips. "Point taken. I'd rather be inside, as well. The smell of horse poop almost makes me puke."

"We gather where we feel most comfortable."

Norma nodded. "We don't have these big dinners often, so it's a nice time for the moms and kids to visit and play."

Reid was quiet for a moment. "Well, as long as you're not in here because it's *expected* of you, I guess it's okay."

When the dishes were washed and the kitchen cleaned, Norma put on coffee and tea and ushered everyone to the large living room.

"Do the dogs have names?" Reid lowered to the floor next to Elise and the other children.

"They do," Norma said with a chuckle, "but they all look so similar, it's hard to tell them apart. Usually it's just 'the dogs' because where one is, they all are."

Seven-year-old Elise climbed onto Reid's lap. If anyone noticed the look of shock and fear on his face, they were kind enough not to mention it.

"The one that is a little bit smaller than the rest is Louise." Elise pointed. "The others are Donald, Daisy, Huey, and Dewey. Donald has a tiny spot on his forehead. Huey has a light part on his belly. And Daisy's back foot has a little blonde on it."

"Donald, Daisy, Huey, Dewey, and Louise? That's awesome; all named after cartoon ducks. I think I'll call them the duck dogs." Reid laughed.

"We didn't want to name the last little girl Louie, so we went with Louise," Elise explained. "I like *the duck dogs*." She smiled.

"You know their names really well. How did you learn them all?" Reid jostled Elise.

"I play with them all the time." Elise giggled. "My dad says maybe I can have a dog when I'm older. And when we don't have to worry about the baby crawling around and grabbing the dog's tail. But me and Zeke think we should get a dog now. A big ol' dog. It could help on the ranch and be a guard dog. We think a black Lab would be best. And we'd name it Bandit and it would wear a red handkerchief around its neck."

"Not that she's thought about it at all," Shay spoke from the couch with a laugh.

"I bet this crew here loves that you come play with them." Reid reached to pet Dewey.

Ezekiel popped his head into the room and pointed to his phone. "Um, Reid? Walker wants you out in the barn office. Says I can show you the way if you don't remember."

Reid scowled, but lifted Elise from his lap and stood. "I'll take the escort if you don't mind."

Zeke nodded.

"Thanks so much for dinner and the great company." Reid waved at the ladies.

"Actually, we'll walk out with you," Shay said as she stood from the couch. "Come on," she motioned to Elise, "let's head home. Give the pups love."

As they trooped down the main house steps, Elise grabbed Reid's hand. "I'm so glad you're here. I want you to teach me to dance like you're going to teach Norma."

Reid's heart constricted.

"It was very nice meeting you." Shay gave Reid a hug. "It may not be what you're used to, but this place is special. We're all like family here. We really are happy to have you here. Your grandfather was a very generous and kind man, we respected him very much. He basically saved our lives, we owe him everything." She turned to Ezekiel. "Don't stay too late. You've got some homework to finish."

The kid nodded.

"How long have you lived here on the ranch?" Reid asked as they began to walk toward the barn. He held his hand over his nose and groaned. "Ugh, that smell is so nasty. I don't know how you do it."

Ezekiel laughed. "You get used to it. I hated it when I first got here, don't even notice it now." He kicked at a rock in the driveway. "Been here about two years. I've lived with just my sister for a long while now. We used to live with our grandma, but she died. Shay was eighteen so she became my guardian."

Reid glanced at Ezekiel, taking in his deeply tanned skin, crystal blue eyes, and short, curly hair. "How old are you?"

"I'll be eighteen in a few months." He shrugged. "Probably leave here, that's for sure."

"Why? Do you not like it?" Finally, maybe a person who wasn't going to sing the praises of the ranch.

"I like it fine. But I don't really fit in. I'm not white, I'm not black, I'm not Hispanic. And everyone aside from Wes and my sister is either way older than me or way younger than me." The young man bent to pick up a stick. "Plus, how am I ever gonna meet girls?"

Reid whipped his head to frown at Ezekiel. "Girls, huh? I didn't see that one coming."

The kid stopped dead in his tracks and faced Reid. "What the hell is that supposed to mean? Huh?" He shoved at Reid's chest.

"Whoa, relax. My bad. I'm usually very good at recognizing a fellow gay boy. Maybe my skills are messed up because of the damn horse shit." Reid held up his hands. "Really, I'm sorry."

"I'm not gay." Ezekiel growled.

"Okay, like I said, I...," Reid started.

"I'm *not*." Zeke snapped again.

"Dude, there's an old saying about the more you protest and deny, the more guilty you appear." Reid crossed both arms over his chest. "Now, I barely know you, so I'm sorry for making assumptions. But, as a gay man myself, I don't see why you're getting so worked up over my mistake. It's not the end of the world to be gay. In fact, I think it's pretty damn awesome."

Ezekiel's face softened a bit. "Sorry. I just get called gay at school all the time and it sucks."

Reid nodded knowingly. "I get it. I got made fun of so much in school." He put an arm around the kid. "Seriously, though, once I accepted who I am and started loving myself more than I cared about what those assholes thought, my life got better day by day."

"Touching story, bro." Zeke elbowed Reid. "But I'm still not gay."

Reid chuckled. "Okay, okay."

They reached the barn office.

"Can you make it from here?" Zeke asked.

"Yeah." Reid reached for the door. "Hey," he grabbed Zeke's shoulder.

The young man turned.

"I won't be here long, but I'll leave my info in case you ever need a place to stay in California or just someone to talk to, okay?"

"I won't." Ezekiel's chin jutted out. "But thanks for the offer."

Reid pressed his lips together and just nodded before walking into the barn.

He paused and looked to the left. What seemed to be a hundred horses were being tended to in some way for the evening. He shuddered and turned to the right toward Walker's office.

~

"WHAT's the story with Wes and Shay?" Reid plopped down in the chair across the desk from Walker.

Walker simply frowned. "Not really my place to divulge their personal life."

"It's my grandfather's ranch. He knew their story. You know their story. I want to know, as well." Reid jutted his chin.

Walker rolled his eyes. "Funny how you show interest in the ranch when you want something." He shook his head. "Wes and Shay came here when Elise was just a little thing. The ranch where Wes worked in Texas got bought and sold."

"They're both so young. How's he know about horses? And what does Shay do on the ranch?"

"He grew up around horses. He's amazing with them. Good, hard worker." Walker shuffled some papers. "And Shay takes care of Elise and watches some of the other little ones as needed. A lot of the spouses take turns watching the kids, carpooling the older kids to school, grocery shopping, keeping the ranch clean and inviting, up and running basically. A good amount of the ladies do handmade crafts and sell them online. Some choose to homeschool. They all stay very busy and very productive and very important to the ranch."

"What about Ezekiel? He said Shay is his guardian."

Walker nodded. "Yeah, he came with them. He was so very angry when they got here. Still has some issues. Still trying to figure out who he is. Like he can't decide if he's the rough and tough bad boy or the soft and caring good guy."

"Definitely got the vibe he's not sure who he is," Reid agreed. "Why can't he be tough and soft? Rough and caring? Maybe he's stuck because he doesn't fit in one exact category."

"Sounds like you relate?"

Reid shrugged. "I guess I just feel like society is too quick to pigeonhole people. Girls wear pink, boys wear blue. Girls play nice, boys play rough. Girls like to read and write, boys like math and science. Girls like dance, boys like football. Girls like dolls, boys like trucks. No wonder kids are so fucked up trying to figure out who they are."

Walker simply sat quietly.

"It's not the end of the world if a boy likes to wear pink or purple. A girl should be encouraged to love math and science. Some of the best dancers in the world are men. Why shouldn't a boy play with dolls and learn to take care of a baby? He may be a father someday. And I know some girls who could totally kick my ass in every single sport." Reid sighed.

"You're right. I agree completely." Walker leaned back in his seat. "Maybe having you here will be good for Zeke. You're closer to his age than I am. He has Wes and Shay, but he could use a friend." Walker's words were laced with a challenge.

"Well, that's as good of a segue into what we need to

talk about as any, I guess." Reid narrowed his eyes and bit his lip. "Really wish you'd all been total assholes. Would have made this easier."

Walker sighed. "Come on, out with it. I need to know what I'm dealing with here."

## 5

"This will be easier if you could just listen to all I have to say first." Reid frowned. "We can discuss questions and specifics after."

Walker's face held the same frown, but he nodded in agreement.

"So, you knew my grandfather much better than I did seeing as how I never met the man. Maybe all of this will make more sense to you than it does to me since you knew him." Reid shifted in his seat. "Pine Ridge has been in my family for generations."

Walker reclined in the desk chair and steepled his fingers at his chin.

"Growing up, I heard about the ranch, but my dad never spoke of it without a grimace and a few curse words, so I always imagined it as a scary, nightmarish place. As I got older, I simply pictured it as a rundown heap of cows and barns, a waste of space." Reid glanced up from the spot on the desk he'd been staring at and met Walker's gaze.

The cowboy cocked a brow in question.

Reid laughed somewhat wryly. "Don't get all riled up, I know better now."

Walker gestured for him to continue.

"I was vaguely aware that the ranch was always passed down from father to son. That was a fuzzy transaction in a child's mind; I sometimes imagined my unknown grandfather handing a large barn to my father. 'Here, son, this is yours now.' Of course, I later realized it had to do with transferring ownership and a lot of legalities and paperwork." Reid paused for a moment. "None of this registered much in my mind because I was a thousand percent certain that when my dad became owner of the ranch he'd sell it in a nanosecond if not quicker."

Walker closed his eyes and pinched the bridge of his nose.

"After my grandpa died," Reid began.

"You know," Walker interrupted, "he would have been so very happy to hear you call him Grandpa Jack."

Reid scowled briefly. "I didn't even know the man."

Walker shrugged. "He knew you and was so proud of you."

Reid shook his head. "Fine. When *Grandpa Jack* died, the family was called in for a reading of the will."

He stopped in his story for a moment. "You know, I always thought a reading of a will sounded so proper and fancy, but it was really pretty tedious and boring. Anyway, my boyfriend at the time, if you could even call him that, was stoked I asked him to attend. He touted this and that about all *we* could do with my inheritance. I didn't want to burst his bubble, but since I'd never met Grandpa Jack, I had very little hope that he was leaving me anything."

Walker shifted, leaning forward in his chair to prop his elbows on the desk as Reid's story continued.

"And I was right," Reid went on, "he didn't leave me a single cent. I'm honestly surprised Jeremy didn't get up and walk out of the room as soon as he realized I wasn't getting a dime." He worried his bottom lip with his teeth. "Well, I guess that's not an entirely accurate statement. Jack left me something of value, I just don't get the money. Yet."

Walker's eyes grew wide. "He left you the ranch?"

Reid nodded.

"What about the tradition of leaving it to the first-born son?" Shock and confusion mixed with dismay on Walker's face.

"I guess Grandpa Jack wasn't one to go along with something just for the sake of tradition. His will stated that he knew his son had always despised the ranch and wouldn't want to burden him with the responsibility." Reid chuckled. "You should have seen my dad. Sputtering, face red, demanding something be done about the injustice. He yelled and slammed things, swore he had always held the ranch in a special place in his heart and wanted nothing more than to inherit part of his father's life."

Walker snorted. "From what I've been told, your father wasn't the least bit interested in the ranch or in his parents, especially his father."

Reid nodded. "Right. And it seems like Grandpa Jack knew that and anticipated what Dad would do with the ranch."

"But isn't that exactly what you're also going to do?" Walker's voice took on a hard edge.

Reid's shoulders slumped. "Well, the will stated that the ranch would remain as part of Jack's possessions for three months. During those three months, I am *required* to live full-time on the ranch. At the end of three months, I can do one of three things. Allow the ranch to be sold and take one hundred percent of the profits. Allow the ranch to be sold and split half of the profits among ranch employees as I see fit. Or keep the ranch in the family and take over ownership. At that point, the will specifies that I could be an owner in name only and leave the running of the ranch to a person of my choice."

Walker bowed his head and clasped both hands at the back of his neck. Taking a deep breath, he finally glanced up at Reid. "Well, which option are you leaning toward?"

"I haven't decided."

"Don't bullshit me," Walker bit out the words. "This affects the lives and futures of every single person on this ranch, including me. I think it's only fair that you let me know what we're facing."

"Look, I'm not lying to you." Reid sighed. "Up until the moment I stepped foot on the ranch, I would have unequivocally said I was going to spend the three months, sell the ranch, and take the money. No questions asked."

"And now?"

"Now. Well, now none of the options sound particularly great." Reid rubbed a hand over his face. "I get it, man. The people here count on the ranch. I'm not a terrible monster, I don't want to rob them of their jobs and their lives."

"What about option four? Take over ownership and leave. Let me run the place. How does that hurt anyone?"

Reid pulled his knees up in the chair and held them against his chest. "This is the part where I get angry at my grandfather for putting me in this position. First, what the hell do I know about picking a good person to run the ranch? Second, that option leaves me without anything other than maybe the interest coming from ranch operations." He pressed his forehead against his knees. "I feel like a total asshole saying that, but I'd like to be out from underneath my parents and the sale of the ranch would allow me to do that."

"Then take over the ranch and live here!" Walker thundered.

Reid scoffed, his words muffled into his legs. "Yeah, gay boy turned cowboy. I'm sure that would work out just fabulously." He lifted his head. "I have no clue how to run a ranch. I stick out like a sore thumb. I'm scared to death of horses. I gag at the smells. And what exactly would I do with my time? Why should I be punished just so others can have a good life?"

Walker raised his brows.

"Yes, I realize how fucking pathetic and selfish that sounds." Reid pressed his head against his knees again. "Damn Grandpa Jack all to hell and back. He should have just left the damn ranch to my dad and kept me out of his life completely."

Walker was quiet for a moment. "Ever think that maybe Grandpa Jack had hopes that you'd fall in love with this place?"

Reid raised his head. "Well, his hopes and dreams are going to shatter like glass. I'm not him. He grew up on this ranch. Loved it from the time he was old enough to understand it was going to become his. He was a horse man, a ranch man, a man who appreciated nature and the great outdoors. I'm none of that."

"How do you know?"

Reid snorted. "Just look at me."

"No, I mean, how do you know all of those things about your grandfather?" Walker cocked his head.

"Easy. I took pretty much everything that's the opposite of me and applied it to him." Reid shrugged. "I am terrified of horses. Nature makes me shiver; bugs and wild animals? No thanks. I don't love the outdoors; give me the mall or a dance studio any day."

Walker leaned back and steepled his fingers under his chin again and watched Reid. "It's a challenge, but I accept."

"Accept what?" Reid frowned.

"I've got three months to convince you to stay or at least leave the day-to-day stuff to me." Walker gave a wan smile. "This ranch is my life. My heart is here. It's the horses, the people, the land. I can't leave here. And it's my responsibility to save the others' jobs. So I accept the challenge."

Reid dropped his knees and leaned forward, elbows on the desk. "Look, I know this place is important to you. I know it's your life and their lives." He gestured vaguely toward the rest of the barn. "But I've got to take care of me. I'm not going to banish myself to living a life of misery on a ranch just to save others. If that makes me selfish, so be it."

"Then go back to California and let me run the place," Walker implored. "I'm the best at what I do. I've been here over a decade. I knew your grandpa. This ranch is in my blood. I'd never do anything to compromise its reputation or operations."

Reid shook his head. "And I get what from that? A small chunk of change every so often from the interest? I can't imagine this place is making more than enough to pay employees and keep things running. Why should I be left with next to nothing so you and they get their dreams?"

"Give me three months, okay? Maybe you'll feel better about your options. Or at least feel different about them." Walker stood from his chair. "Can you give me three months of an open mind?"

Reid nodded and stood, as well. "I have no choice but to give you three months." He squinted. "But tell me the truth, you'd rather have me hand it all over to you, right?"

Walker cocked his head. "Honestly? I'm not sure. Having the run of the ranch without a damn city slicker around to fuck things up would be great. But I'm a man who likes an adventure, so maybe having you stay would make things a hell of lot more interesting around here." He winked.

Reid laughed. "No promises. But I can give you three months of an open mind. All I've ever wanted was for people to give *me* an open mind and acceptance, so it's the least I can do for you and Pine Ridge."

They shook hands over the desk.

"Come on, we need to head to the main house and

get some sleep. Tomorrow comes early on a ranch."
Walker held open the door for Reid.

Reid's nose crinkled. "Exactly how early is early?"

"Sun up." Walker slapped him on the shoulder as
Reid groaned. "Welcome to ranch life, cowboy."

Reid simply grimaced. "What exactly will we be
doing tomorrow?"

"Nothing fancy, just day-to-day stuff." Walker led
them out of the barn. "I'll start you with things away
from the horses. Let you get a feel for the whole opera-
tion before we tackle anything having to do with
animals."

Reid stopped dead in his tracks. "Hell to the no. I'll
help and learn, but I'm not going near the horses. Ever.
Period."

Walker turned. "They are majestic, caring, sensitive,
and intelligent creatures. Maybe at least give them a
chance?"

"They are huge and they kick. They are dangerous.
I have no need to be near them." Reid crossed both arms
over his chest.

"Fine." Walker turned away, but called over his
shoulder, "So much for that open mind and acceptance.
What if people were as closed off to you as you are to
the horses?"

A horse neighed from the barn behind them.

Reid yelped and ran to catch up with Walker. "I
don't kick and trample and kill," Reid argued.

Walker snorted as they headed up the stairs of the main house. "Neither do most horses. What the hell have you been watching? Horse horror stories?"

Reid jutted his chin and entered the house, dropping to his knees to greet the dogs who clamored across the floor to tackle him.

Walker laughed. "Remember, sun up. Breakfast will be ready, hope you are too."

## 6

*W*alker snickered the next morning as Reid all but dragged himself to the kitchen table and collapsed in a chair the next morning.

"Coffee, in an IV, stat," Reid mumbled into the crook of his elbow not even bothering to lift his head.

Norma sat a large mug of steaming black coffee in front of Reid and patted his shoulder. "Sugar?"

"Hmmm?" Reid muttered.

Walker laughed out loud despite the frown Norma shot his way. "She's not calling *you* sugar, cowboy." He picked up the tray of sugar and cream and placed it on the table. "Sugar?"

Reid lifted his head and squinted his eyes as if waking from a long nap. "It's still dark outside. How is a person supposed to function like this?" He reached for the sugar and put in two heaping spoons and a splash of cream.

"Want a little coffee with your sugar?" Walker teased.

"Don't start, Mr. I-Like-My-Cream-Flavored-with-Coffee," Norma scolded and poked Walker in the chest as she went back to preparing breakfast.

By the time food was served, Reid had consumed two cups of coffee and the duck dogs had given up begging at his chair and lay down nearby. He spooned homestyle potatoes onto his plate and accepted the basket of piping hot biscuits Walker handed his way. With a slab of salt-cured ham and a generous helping of scrambled cheese eggs on his plate, Reid glanced around the table at Walker and Norma. "You guys seriously do this every damn day?"

Norma nodded. "Wouldn't have it any other way. Nothing I like better than rising in time to get a meal prepared and enjoy a hot cup of coffee as the sun comes up."

"I let you sleep in today," Walker joked. "Should have been out at the barn an hour ago."

Reid's eyes widened. "Wow, you must *really* want me to leave." He shot a look toward Norma.

"I know all about your three month stay and the decisions you need to make." Norma reached over and patted his hand. "I plan to have you so smitten with this place that you'll not even be able to think of a time when you didn't want to spend your every waking moment here."

Reid smiled. "I can't promise anything. Take the boy from the city, not the city from the boy and whatnot." He gestured with a biscuit. "But this food is a damn good start to making me want to never leave."

"Norma's cooking is legendary." Walker poured himself more coffee from the carafe and doctored it with cream and a half spoon of sugar.

"What do the others eat?" Reid buttered another biscuit before shoveling in more eggs.

"Many eat at home. Some, mostly the ones who stay on the property, will do their early chores then come up for breakfast before continuing their day." Walker forked open two biscuits and placed a piece of ham into each. "We need to head out as soon as you finish. But bring a couple sandwiches to eat. You'll be starving by lunch."

"This was carb loading at its most delicious. I don't think I'll be hungry again even by dinner time," Reid argued, but he made himself two ham biscuits, as well, wrapping them in a napkin, before draining his coffee. "Norma, can I help in any way?"

"Mighty kind offer, sugar," Norma teased and Walker laughed, "but the kitchen and house are my job, and what I do best. I'll be fine. Bring your appetite for lunch, though. Beef Manhattans and three types of pie are on the menu."

Reid groaned and followed Walker to the door.

Walker pulled on boots and a hat before giving Reid's denim joggers and fitted T-shirt a once over. "You got anything to cover your head? The sun can be brutal."

Reid wrinkled his nose. "I don't have a hat."

"What about boots?" Walker put both hands on his hips. "And not those damn excuses for boots you were wearing when I picked you up."

Reid copied Walker's stance and jutted his chin. "Those boots were beautiful. Maybe not the best for working," he argued.

Walker cocked a brow.

"Okay, maybe not the best for walking, either." Reid gave in with a huff. "But it's not like I had a ton of time or knowledge to get myself all cowboy'd up before I came out here."

"Fine, we'll get you a hat and boots soon." Walker groused. "Until then, do you have shoes you can get dirty? And anything to cover your head?"

"I'll improvise." Reid shrugged and walked to his room. He emerged a few moments later with high-top tennis shoes and a rainbow bandana covering his head as he sauntered down the hallway like he was on a catwalk. "Better?"

Walker harrumphed and nodded.

"Geesh, you'd think you're the fashion police." Reid patted Walker's cheek. "Can't be out and about on my first day looking like a scrub. I still gotta represent and part of that means looking *fine* all the time." He walked through the door and bounded down the steps. "Where to first?"

Walker followed, shaking his head. "Well, one of the first things you need to know is how to drive the truck."

Reid tossed Walker a sneer. "I know how to *drive*. Check that off the list. Next?"

Walker rolled his eyes and walked toward a beat-up truck. "That may be, but this here is Bert and he's a bitch even on his best days."

Reid curled his lip. "Ugh, Bert, why you gotta be a diva?" He patted the truck. "Although, if he kept me looking as rough as he's let you get, I'd probably be bitchy, too." Reid turned to Walker. "A little maintenance never hurts."

"I'll keep that in mind." Walker smirked. "You know how to drive a stick?"

Reid batted his lashes slowly. "Oh, yeah, I know *exactly* how to drive a stick."

Walker cocked a brow. "Really?"

"Mmmhmm," Reid purred. "I can work a stick over, front and back, up and down. By the time I'm done, that stick won't know what day it is."

Walker's eyes snapped with a fiery glow before his jaw clenched. "Fucking, hell. I mean a stick shift...in a vehicle...a manual...the opposite of an automatic transmission," Walker sputtered.

Reid winked. "I know. But that was fun."

Walker huffed. "We don't have time for this. I'm already behind schedule. Do you or do you not know how to drive a manual transmission?"

"Touchy, touchy," Reid murmured. "I have driven a stick, a *manual*, before, but it's been a very long time. Is Bert temperamental?"

"Yes, the worst." Walker opened the truck door. "But, I make all the employees know how to drive Bert in case of emergencies. Climb in." Walker waited until Reid had shut the driver side door before walking around to the passenger side. "Start the bastard up." Walker gave a nod toward the keys.

Bert roared to life and shook softly.

"Oh, Berty, you are just a hunk of lovin' aren't you, big guy?" Reid ran one hand over the steering wheel and the other across the faded gray upholstery. "You just need a man who can handle all that power. I'm your boy, Berty, I gotchu, Boo."

Walker cleared his throat. "You done?"

"What?" Reid shrugged. "You can't expect me to just climb in and drive him. He needs prepping and pampering, too. I mean, if I'm going to get anywhere with Bert, I need to lube him up, I can't go trying to fuck him dry."

Walker pinched the bridge of his nose. "Bert is a truck, not a trick."

Reid's mouth dropped open and he held a hand to

his chest, gasping. "Did you seriously just insinuate that I'm a hooker?"

Walker held up a hand. "I'm sorry. I didn't mean to offend. I just need you to know how to drive the damn truck. And...," he let his word trail off.

"And what?" Reid demanded.

"And if you could possibly not make every single thing we talk about today an innuendo, that would be great." Walker raised his brow, waiting.

"Sorry," Reid mumbled. "I'm sassy and smart-assy, especially when I'm nervous or stressed. I'll try not to be so raunchy. I didn't mean to offend your delicate hetero-senses. My bad."

Walker frowned, but quickly went on, nodding. "Thanks. That would be great. Let's take a few rounds in Bert and then get to the other chores."

"Grab your grub, if you want." Walker indicated the napkin-wrapped biscuits on the truck seat. "You can eat while we watch the men turn out the horses."

Reid reached for his food, but his wide eyes flashed to Walker. "Told you I don't do horses."

"If you're going to be on a ranch, whether three months or forever, you gotta get used to them." Walker climbed from the truck and met Reid at the driver's side. "I ain't asking you to saddle one up and ride."

Reid sighed and glanced at Walker for a brief moment before jerking his gaze away. *Do **not** think about riding him. Just don't.*

"Yet," Walker amended and chuckled at Reid's glare. "But you need to see how things work around here, and get to know the guys."

Reid bit into a biscuit. "So why do none of the women work out here?" he asked as he chewed.

Walker shrugged. "Just never been that way. The men work out here, and the women work in the houses with the others and help with the kids."

Reid narrowed his eyes. "What if Elise gets her daddy's skill with horses? You gonna expect her to cook and clean or you gonna let her work with the horses?"

Walker frowned. "You make it sound like I'm some old-fashioned, misogynist."

"If the boot fits," Reid drawled.

"When I started running things, I pretty much allowed the ranch to run as it had been. If it ain't broke, don't fix it, ya know?"

Reid popped the last bite of biscuit in his mouth and chewed. "Well, if I stay, things are gonna change around here."

"You gonna *make* the women work out here?" Walker scowled.

"No, but it should be an option." Reid folded his arms over his chest. "And if any of the guys have an interest in creating items to sell, running errands,

helping with the cooking, taking on some of the respon-
sibilities with the kids, then it should be a choice." His
jaw clenched as he waited for Walker's reply.

Walker shrugged and held up his hands. "I'm not
against it. I won't fight you."

Reid's shoulders relaxed, and he nodded. "Good."
He glanced at the barn. "Fine, show me around and
teach me oh, wise one."

They walked to the barn and stood at the corral as
the men let the horses out to run.

"So, they just stay in this fence all day?" Reid wrinkled his nose as pounding hooves kicked up dust.

"No, some will be exercised while others are let out
to pasture to graze and walk. Some are used for ranch
chores. Some will be working with a trainer. They all get
something different, but exactly what they need. And it
varies day-to-day." Walker lifted a hand in greeting to
the men with the horses. "Don't worry. They are all *very*
well taken care of. Your grandfather put the top priority
on the horses. It's one of the ways he turned this place
into what it is today. He took his business mind, and
added it to his work ethic, his integrity, and his kind
heart, and made Pine Ridge into something to be
proud of."

"Do all the employees have one job they do all the
time or does it change up?" Reid rested his elbows on
the fence.

"Just depends on what needs done." Walker

pushed his hat up on his forehead a bit. "Wes works the most one-on-one with the new horses, the ones needing broken or rehabilitated or trained. I work a lot with the horses, but Wes is a master. The other guys do whatever needs to be done. Mucking the stalls, mending fences, running into town for supplies, baling hay and all that goes along with it, helping if a foal is on its way, painting sheds, moving the small herd of cattle from pasture to shelter and back to pasture. The ranch jobs are never ending; definitely never going to be bored."

Reid gasped and his entire face softened. "Ohhhh, look at them."

Walker turned to see the foals emerging from the barn and beginning to frolic in the corral. "Well, lookie there, maybe you don't hate *all* horses."

"*Those* aren't horses, those are babies, and they are cute as fuck." Reid moved to the other side of Walker to get a better view of the young ones.

"All big horses start out looking *cute as fuck*." Walker chuckled. "We'll start you with the foals and move from there."

Over the next hour, Reid was introduced to and chatted with most all of the men. Some lived on the ranch, and some commuted to the ranch daily. A few he remembered from dinner, but he worked hard to learn and retain their names.

"Hey, Wes, think this little filly would be a good one

to break-in Reid?" Walker hollered across the corral to Wes while pointing at a foal.

"Yeah, she's super sweet and loves attention," Wes hollered and waved back.

The rest of the horses were out of the corral or being tended to so Walker opened the gate. "Come on. Time to meet your nemesis."

"She's not my nemesis, her mother and father are." Reid grimaced and looked toward the other horses. "Are they going to see me with her and come running to protect her?"

Walker laughed. "Nah, her mom is out in the pasture. Her dad isn't here. He was sold before she was born."

"That's cruel. You sold her dad? So she'll never know him?" Reid stepped forward and let Walker close the gate behind him. *Don't notice the soft gruffness of his laugh.*

"That's the way it works. She's got her mom. That's who she needs most. But soon she'll be completely independent. Even if her mom wasn't here, the others, especially the older mares who have had foals, would take her in and teach her." Walker clicked his tongue and held out a hand toward the baby then turned to Reid. "Hold your hand out and let her sniff you."

Reid did as he was told, and the foal nudged his hand and bumped his chest with her head. "Hey, careful." Reid's voice shook, but he stood his ground.

"She's wanting you to pet her." Walker scratched the horse on her jaw and down her long face.

"Funny way of asking," Reid grumbled but stroked the filly's nose. "She's so soft, and her nose feels like velvet."

The foal nuzzled against Reid's side.

"She likes you," Walker stated.

When a large horse was led to another part of the corral, Reid opted to end the foal love-fest. Walker locked the gate behind them, and the men stood outside the fence as the foal scampered off to play with her buddies.

"Holy shit," Reid drawled.

"What?" Walker looked his way.

"You must be magic." Reid shook his head.

"How's that?"

"I swore I'd *never* get near a horse ever again. Ever. Again. And you just had me *touching* one." Reid rested a hand on top of his head.

Walker winked. "Nah, no magic. Just the adorable-ness of a filly." He turned toward the barn. "I'll show you the tack and feed areas."

As the men left the corral, Walker cleared his throat. "So, what happened to make you so scared of horses?"

Reid's lip curled. "Went riding at a park when I was little. They put me on one of the tallest, biggest horses. Supposedly he was the calmest, but he was scary as fuck. When we were on the trail in the woods, one of the other horses came up beside my horse, and ran us into a tree. So my leg was trapped between the horse and the tree. My horse stumbled, I scraped my arm and leg against the tree, and then I fell off. The falling part was likely my fault because I let go and tried to get off. But the whole situation scared the ever-loving shit out of me. I vowed to never go near a horse again." Reid huffed. "Which wasn't hard living where I did. But living on a horse ranch is going to make that a bit of a bitch to stick to, ya know?"

"Well, three months isn't that long. You can probably avoid the horses most of the time." Walker glanced over at Reid.

Reid gave a wan smile. "Yeah, that's true. But I'd hate to miss out on petting...wait, what's her name?"

"Haven't named her yet, actually."

"Cinnamon. Her fur looks like the color of cinnamon." Reid frowned. "That doesn't seem right, what's a horse's fur actually called?"

"Her coat," Walker answered. "You're right, though. She's definitely cinnamon colored. Cinnamon it is."

Reid smiled.

"I think that was your first official act on the ranch." Walker swung the door open. "We let the horses graze in the pasture, but not for long periods of time. We keep them healthy with hay and grain feed. The hay is kept in the loft and some down here on the floor. The grain feed is kept in these large cans. We can't really keep mice out of the hay, but we keep the grain sealed to keep the critters out. It's important to keep the hay and grain dry."

Reid grimaced as he glanced at the hay. "There's mice in there?"

"Likely." Walker chuckled. "We have four or five cats on the ranch, so they help to keep the rodents at bay."

Reid shuddered. "I don't really like cats, but if they keep the mice away I guess I can deal."

"The ranch cats aren't all that friendly. They roam around, and we keep them fed, but they aren't super social." Walker led the way to a small room in the barn. "This is the tack room."

Reid popped his head into the room. "Ohhh, it smells good in here. Like leather. I like this room."

Walker laughed. "I guess I know where to find you if you ever go missing. Maybe you can help out with oiling the leather."

Reid pretended to toss hair off his shoulders. "Girl, I'm a pro at oiling things up."

Walker stared at Reid for a moment and then shook his head. "Just couldn't help yourself, huh?"

Reid's cheeks pinked. "Sorry."

"No worries. I walked right into it." Walker winked and cleared his throat. *Do not think about oiling him up. Jesus, man, get it together.* "Let's head to the garage. We'll take the four-wheelers out. I'll show you cows and some of the fences on the property lines."

"Four-wheelers?" Reid clasped his hands together. "That's the first thing you've said that I've been totally down with."

Walker smiled. "Let's go then, cowboy."

"Yee-haw," Reid drawled.

## 7

*R*eid sneezed as they walked back through the barn. "Eeeww, what are they doing?"

Walker glanced toward where Reid was looking. "Mucking out the stalls."

"So, like, scooping poop?" Reid held a hand over his mouth. "Gross. I choose to never do that job. I'm high enough up to make that choice, right?"

Walker laughed. "Sure, big guy. You don't have to scoop poop."

Reid sneezed again. "Gah, my nose and throat are itching like crazy."

When they left the barn and headed toward the garage, Reid sneezed five more times.

"Damn, man. Let me see your eyes." Walker reached for Reid's arm.

Reid turned after sneezing again.

"Your eyes are red and watery. Sneezing. Itchy nose and throat. You must be allergic to something." Walker reached into his pocket. "Here you can take this for now. We'll get you some allergy meds in town."

Reid popped open the packet and swallowed the pill.

"Dang, I could have gotten you some water." Walker laughed.

"I'm used to swallowing things down." Reid winked.

Walker rolled his eyes.

"What do you think I'm allergic to?"

"Could be anything. Grass, horses, hay, dust? Who knows." Walker shrugged. "You'll want to be sure to shower and wash your hair really well each evening. Norma will give you some allergy meds until we get into town and get you something from Doc."

"Doc? You get medication from someone named Doc?" Reid pinched the bridge of his nose. "My entire face feels like it's about to catch fire any second, I'm likely allergic to ninety percent of my surroundings, and you want me to take medications from some guy named Doc? Fuck my life."

"You can wash your face at the garage. Doc is a female. And you won't be here long, so no worries." Walker slapped Reid on the back.

"Gee, thanks." Reid huffed. "Your bedside manner sucks."

"Don't go getting all excited, because this one's an automatic," Walker drawled as he patted the seat of a four-wheeler.

Reid smirked and dried his freshly washed face on a towel. "Shame," he purred.

"You feel any better?" Walker opened the smaller garage door on the side.

"Face isn't so itchy." Reid swallowed. "Throat is maybe a little better. Hope that medicine is non-drowsy."

"Pretty much. I take it quite often, and I don't get tired." Walker climbed on a second four-wheeler and indicated Reid should climb on the other.

"Yeah, but you also get up at the ass crack of dawn so I'm not sure your definition of drowsy is the same as mine." Reid tossed the towel at the sink and straddled the ATV.

Walker laughed. "We won't be going terribly fast, but grab a helmet if you want one." He pointed to the wall of helmets.

Reid shrugged off the suggestion.

"You know how to drive one of these, right? It's pretty much like a golf cart or similar."

"I'll excuse the insinuation that I'm a golfer," Reid quipped. "As long as I can get it started, I'm sure I can drive it."

"Okay, stay beside or behind me. We'll go to the property line." Walker pointed to the key, started up his machine and waited for Reid to do the same.

They traveled first over mostly flat, dusty land, steering clear of driving through the grass area.

Walker slowed to a stop and pointed. "There's our herd. Not large at all. Enough to provide some beef every once in a while, but we still have to buy meat. Norma uses the dairy cow milk whenever she can, but still has to supplement with store-bought. She's been hounding me to get a few more dairies so we can use only our own milk. We'll see."

"So they just roam around eating?" Reid watched the quiet, doe-eyed cattle chew the grass.

"They get to graze, which is what they really like, but we feed them grain to fill in nutrition, as well. This area isn't super lush for grazing. We rotate them so they aren't always grazing in the same spots." Walker pointed to the horizon. "See that tree over there? That's the edge of the property. We'll ride the fence and check for breaches."

The terrain became rockier and rougher as they drove away from the cattle. Soon they reached a lone tree just inside a fence line.

Reid glanced around. "Not very exciting. I guess I thought there'd be signs or something."

Walker laughed. "The fence is our sign. Obviously this isn't the only property edge. But this is the closest one. So, we'll drive back toward the house, but stick to the fence line. We're looking for broken posts, cut or bent wire, or any spot that looks different."

The men rode along the fence until the house was in sight. Only the sound of the motors broke the silence of the wide-open space.

Walker halted the vehicles with a raised hand and shut off his engine.

Reid followed suit.

"See anything amiss here?" Walker spread out his hands and indicated a large area of fence.

Reid scanned the posts and wires. "That post is split in two and the wire looks loose."

"Good, I'll make a rancher of you yet," Walker teased. "So, myself or others will come out here and fix that up within twenty-four to forty-eight hours. We don't want to leave it like this. It's a risk of entry, a risk of injury, but most importantly a risk of one of our animals getting out."

Reid was quiet for a moment while the sounds of nature filled the air.

"Doesn't this ever get old?" Reid asked. "Being out in the middle of nowhere, same people, same work, same everything?"

Walker was silent as he gazed at the vast openness around him. "Nah, man. It's beautiful, peaceful, and truly never gets boring. Plus, we're not *that* far from town. I'll take you there soon. Show you around. Movie theaters, stores, restaurants, and bars. Bet we can even find you somewhere to dance if we ask the right people."

"What about your love life? How are you going to meet someone? Do you have a lady friend on the ranch?" Reid turned on his seat and pulled one knee up and under his leg.

Walker frowned. "I don't date."

"Why?"

"Tried it, bad ending, so I just don't date." Walker clenched his jaw.

"Cheating? Bad breakup? They didn't like ranch life?" Reid shifted his knee to his chest and propped his chin on it.

"Not that it's any of your business, but it just ended badly. Too many feelings, too hard in the end." Walker scowled. "I've got all I need here on the ranch, so I'm not missing out."

"What about sex?"

"What about it? Sex isn't everything in life," Walker grumbled.

"True, but sex can be good. And just having someone to share with and be close to..."

"I've got friends here on the ranch I can share with," Walker bit out and shut down any further conversation by starting the ATV's engine and waving to Reid.

By the time the sun started to set, Reid was about to drop. Lunch had been a boisterous and enjoyable affair, and Reid had longed to sneak off to his room to cuddle the puppies and take a nap. But Walker had declared they would be unloading hay after lunch and didn't allow Reid the escape he so desperately wanted.

With the beginning of blisters on his hands, despite the work gloves Walker had given him, and every part of him damp with sweat or exhausted or both, Reid followed Walker to the barn office and collapsed into a chair. "Please tell me this day is almost done."

Walker laughed. "Most evenings I try to get about an hour of paperwork completed. Just to stay caught up. It sucks, but it's worse if I let it go."

"What kind of paperwork?" Reid cracked an eye while resting his head on the chair back.

"Bills, payroll, accounting for supplies we've used and what we need." Walker ticked items off on his fingers. "Notes on the livestock, correspondence with people wanting to use our services, purchase or sell a horse, just to name a few."

"Sounds like a barrel of fun," Reid drawled.

"It's all part of the job." Walker shrugged and started tapping keys on the computer. "I could hire it out," he began.

"Seems like it's better to keep it in-house if possible," Reid commented. "I mean, safer? Make sure it's done right?"

"Yeah, that's what Jack always said." Walker nodded. "Sounds like you've got more of Jack in you than you think." He smiled as he continued typing.

Reid scoffed. "Whatever." He leaned forward. "Anything I can do to help? I'm pretty good with numbers and spreadsheets."

Walker set Reid up to enter paid bills into a spreadsheet. They worked comfortably for about forty-five minutes, a few comments and questions here and there. Within the hour, they finished their work.

"Please, dear lord, tell me it's time to go to bed?" Reid groaned as he stood and stretched.

"Yeah, definitely bedtime." Walker yawned.

They walked toward the house. The pack of dogs met them at the door, and Reid bent to give them pets and loving. Once inside, he straightened and kicked off his shoes. "What's on the agenda tomorrow?"

"Rise at ass crack o'clock," Walker teased with a wink, "breakfast, strong coffee, chores and that fence. Then I think we better make a trip to town. We'll see if Zeke wants to go."

"Ohhh, road trip." Reid clasped his hands together.

"Get some sleep, cowboy. We work before we play." Walker slapped Reid on the back.

"All work and no play makes Jack a dull boy," Reid pouted, quoting the old proverb.

"Maybe makes *Jack* a dull boy, but builds character for Reid," Walker quipped. "And I'm pretty sure you're at no risk of ever becoming *dull*."

Reid smiled and batted his lashes before executing a

dramatic bow. "Why, thank you, kind sir. And with that compliment, I bid you adieu."

Walker snorted. "G'night, kid."

The pack of pups followed Reid all the way to his room and disappeared behind the door into their new favorite sleeping location.

Walker headed to his room. Behind his closed door, he studied himself in the mirror and ran a hand over his face. "Never been jealous of a bunch of dogs before tonight," he muttered to the room. The large kind-size bed had never looked so empty.

## 8

*R*eid looked around. "So, this is "town,"
huh?"

Zeke curled his lip. "Yep, this is it."

"I'm going to leave you two to shop for clothes,
shoes, and a hat." Walker pulled into a parking spot and
turned off the truck. "I'll go gather the odds and ends we
need before our next big order goes in." He looked at his
watch. "Let's meet back here in two hours. We'll grab
lunch before Reid's appointment with Doc." Walker
turned and headed down the street.

Reid nodded then faced Zeke. "It's not too terrible,
honestly. Looks like a nice place. Not at all run-down
like I was thinking. Definitely looks like it's got more
than one stoplight." He gazed from left to right. "Yeah, I
can work with this."

"For now, right?" Zeke asked. "I mean, you only

have to work with it for three months. Think about those of us facing a lifetime here."

"Oh, well, yeah." Reid raised and lowered a shoulder. "I mean, it's not like I'll be here forever."

Zeke grunted.

"Okay, where should we start?" Reid rubbed his hands together. "I love a good shopping trip."

"Simmer down there, man." Zeke chuckled. "We're not on Rodeo Drive."

"Doesn't matter. I love shopping. *And* I get to try some new styles, so I'm extra excited." Reid used both hands to point left and right. "Which way?"

Zeke shook his head and pointed across the street. "We'll start over there. You're gonna need jeans, boots, shirts, and a hat. Probably socks too so the boots don't rub your shins."

An hour and a half later, Reid and Zeke, loaded down with bags, headed back toward the truck.

"Dude, I don't know how the hell you made getting some clothes seem like such an event. Like, most people go in, grab some jeans and a shirt, and they're done." Zeke glanced down at the bags he was carrying. "You made it an extravaganza. Like it was fun."

"That's because it *is* fun." Reid spun the bags around as he twirled down the sidewalk. "*Work jeans* don't have to be boring. Shirts can have some pizzazz. Boots can *look* just as good as they work. And if you're wearing a hat, you should make it a statement."

"Well, I gotta say, I've never seen someone make trying on clothes so interesting." Zeke laughed. "You'll be the best dressed person on the ranch, that's for sure."

"Might as well feel good and look good while you're working." Reid shrugged. "Plus, I've got to keep up my reputation. I can't go around looking sloppy. Even when lounging, one can look *fine*."

They reached the truck and found Walker waiting.

He whistled. "Damn, did you buy them out?"

"Almost," Zeke said.

"What? They had nice stuff, and it looked good." Reid shrugged. "Go big or go home, that's my motto." He grinned.

"Any problem using the card I gave you?" Walker helped load the bags into the truck.

"Nope," Reid popped the *p* in the word.

"That's because he only used it for like a third of what he bought," Zeke tattled.

"What?" Walker frowned. "Why?"

"I used the card for the items I *needed*. I used my own money for the items I *wanted*." Reid shoved two more bags at Walker. "I'll give you a fashion show when we get home. Some of these jeans make my ass look completely edible." He fluttered his lashes.

Walker groaned and Reid cackled.

"Tell him." Reid turned to Zeke.

Eyes wide, Zeke stuttered, "Tell him what?"

"That my ass looks amazing in some of the jeans." Reid folded both arms over his chest.

Zeke stammered. "I mean, yeah, the jeans fit well if that's what you mean."

"It's not, but whatever," Reid quipped. "Let's get lunch. I'm starving."

The small mom-and-pop diner boasted homemade dishes, the best cup of coffee, and pie to die for. When the three men left, their hunger fed and then some, they made their way to the small building that housed the town doctor.

"I've already told them to bill the ranch if there's anything your insurance doesn't cover." Walker stopped in front of the doctor's office. "I've got one more stop to make. I'll see ya at the truck in a bit. We can pick up any prescriptions Doc gives you and then we'll head home."

The waiting room held one very pregnant woman, an older gentleman, and a man with an icepack on his arm. Reid signed in and took a seat as far from the others as possible. Zeke sat next to him.

"Can I ask you something?" Zeke's voice was low.

"Shoot." Reid glanced at the kid.

"Doesn't it bother you? Being so out and matter-of-fact about being gay?" Zeke whispered, his tone indicating just how incredulous he must be feeling.

"Not at all." Reid shook his head.

"But, like, everyone at the ranch knows you're gay.

How do you deal with that? Don't you feel like people are always watching you, judging you?" Zeke frowned.

"Does it bother you that everyone knows you're straight?" Reid bumped Zeke's shoulder.

Zeke screwed up his face. "No, man. Straight is *normal*." He air-quoted the word.

"Well, gay is my normal. I got tired of lying to myself, lying to others. It was exhausting trying to convince myself I'd eventually find the perfect girl and finally feel the way toward her that I already knew I felt toward guys." Reid turned in his seat and pulled a knee up to his chest.

A door opened and a nurse emerged. "Mr. Keyes? Come on back."

The man with the icepack stood up.

"How you doing today?" the nurse asked.

"Been better. Working in the fencerow and something stung me, maybe bit me, don't know. Swelled up like a melon." The man followed the nurse through the door.

Reid shivered. "Ugh, nature. See? That right there is one reason to stay indoors."

"Kinda hard to do on a ranch," Zeke scoffed. "So, your normal is gay...," he prompted.

"Huh?" Reid turned his attention back to the kid. "Oh, right, gay is my normal. Gay is me. People are going to judge, no matter what. I'd rather be judged while being true to myself than be judged while hiding who I really am."

"What made you finally decide to come out?" Zeke chewed on a nail.

"Boy, don't bite your nails. It's gross and makes them look dreadful." Reid slapped at Zeke's hand. "Honestly? I spent a long time thinking about what it would mean to stay quiet, to fit the mold, to be *normal*, and I realized I just couldn't do it. Because being forty years-old with three kids, a wife, and a secret just didn't seem luxurious. It wasn't how I wanted to live, trapped and hiding. It doesn't work like that for everyone. One of my best friends at the time came out in junior high like it was no big deal. Another casual friend is still hiding, scared to death to be true to himself and admit he's gay."

"What if someone knows it, like deep down, but just can't bring themselves to admit it out loud to people?"

"Each person has to determine what's best for them." Reid gave a sad smile. "If this *hypothetical* person is in danger if he comes out, then keeping the secret is probably best. If he's just worried what people will think?" Reid shrugged. "One, we all need to remember that people likely aren't thinking about us nearly as much as we think they are. Two, he needs to imagine living his entire life with his secret, hiding the true him, and evaluate if that's something he feels he can live with. Three? The best one. You could always let this person know I'm available for Goda services."

Zeke wrinkled his nose. "Goda services? What the

hell does that mean?" His face went stony. "Not that this is a real person, I mean, like...not that I would even be able to tell him, or her...this, I'm just saying what if..."

"Right, right," Reid nodded. "I mean, *if* this person was real, and *if* they were dealing with big realizations and decisions, you could let them know I'm the perfect Goda. That's *gay Yoda.* The Force is strong in this one," Reid pointed at his chest, "and I can guide a new gaybie. Be their support, their wise one, their sage."

Zeke laughed out loud and quickly covered his mouth. "Oh my God. You are such a dork."

"I'm just saying. You could let this person know I'm available to help."

"Reid?" a different nurse opened the door.

Reid stood.

"You won't even be here that long," Zeke grumbled.

"I'll be here for a while." He waved his phone in the air. "And we've got great technology for keeping in touch these days." Reid winked and turned to greet the nurse.

"Hi, Reid Alexander. I'm Doctor Phips." A black woman who immediately reminded Reid of the quintessential grandmother bustled through the door and offered him a hand to shake.

"Hi," Reid replied and shook her hand.

"Well, first, it's great to have you here. I hear you'll be at Pine Ridge for a while?" Dr. Phips flipped through the papers in Reid's folder.

"Yes, three months."

"Only three months?" Dr. Phips looked up. "That seems a shame. Hardly enough time to really learn to love it here."

"Three months is the minimum." Reid shifted in his chair.

"Well, whatever brought you here, whatever you decide to do, keep your mind and your heart open. I think ranch living is good for a person's soul, and the good lord knows you could be good for that ranch." She placed the folder on the counter before washing her hands.

"Not sure how a gay city boy can be good for a ranch," Reid scoffed.

"You hush. I can already tell you've got a great deal to offer. Maybe not so much to the physical ranch, but to the people. You just be you, the rest will happen if it's meant to be." Dr. Phips dried her hands and pulled on some gloves.

"That sounds a bit like a fake fortune teller gazing into a crystal ball." Reid chuckled.

"Just take my word. I see great things happening. And, seeing as I'm a doctor and all, you should trust me." Dr. Phips put the stethoscope in her ears and effectively shut down the conversation by asking Reid to take deep breaths.

Several minutes later, after a thorough exam of his ears, nose, throat, lymph nodes, and lungs, Dr. Phips scribbled notes on Reid's chart before pulling out a prescription pad. "Allergies is my diagnosis. You'll likely get used to most of the things here. Since you stated you've never had allergy problems before, I'm guessing your body is reacting and adjusting to new air, plants, and all the animals." She scribbled on the note pad. "I'll give you two medications. This one, take daily at least until we get a couple good hard freezes. The other one, take if you're having a reaction. Neither should make you super drowsy, but I'd take the daily one at night. Be sure to always shower before bed, making sure to wash your hair so you don't bring allergens to bed."

Reid took both slips of paper. "Sounds good. Thanks."

"You come back if anything is bothering you, understand?" Dr. Phips placed hands on her hips. "Medical/physical stuff, emotional things, social issues, I'm here for all of it."

Reid smiled. "That's good to know." He walked toward the door. "I think I like you. You're a lot nicer and friendlier than any of the doctors I've ever had."

"Well, I *know* I like you." Dr. Phips patted his shoulder. "I think you may just be the answer to some unspoken prayers around these parts."

"I think I'm going to start calling you Dr. Fortune. You're sort of creepy with all that, ya know?" Reid pretended to shiver. "And I'm not the answer to anything, especially prayers, unless the question is, 'Who is the most attractive and stylish gay rancher of them all?'"

Dr. Phips threw her head back and laughed. "You are something else. But don't go thinking you've got that title all wrapped up and won."

Reid frowned. *Who else would wear that title?*

"Now go on, I've got more patients. The world doesn't revolve around you." She shoved him toward the door.

Reid gasped and held a hand to his heart. "What?! Well, I *never!*"

They both laughed as they walked toward the front.

"Head on up to the front desk. They'll take care of you there." Dr. Phips stopped and held out a hand. "It was an *absolute* pleasure." She turned and gathered a folder from the wall at another door before knocking.

Reid smiled and shook his head. Doc Phips certainly was a character.

After settling at the desk, Reid walked out to find Zeke resting his head back against the wall behind his chair. "Ready?"

Zeke jerked his head up. "Huh?" He glanced around. "Oh, yeah, didn't think you'd get done so soon."

"Dude, I was in there over forty minutes. Did you fall asleep?" Reid laughed as they headed out the door.

"No, just thinking," Zeke answered. "Lots of fucking thinking."

Reid smiled at the back of Zeke's head as the kid beelined to the truck.

"You and me both kid," Reid muttered. "But I'm guessing our thoughts are on completely different things."

## 9

After dinner and the evening chores, Norma insisted that Reid show off his new clothes.

"I'm gonna work in the office," Walker snapped.

"No. You're not." Norma pressed on his shoulder and pushed him onto the couch. "You're going to sit here and enjoy the fashion show."

Reid smiled broadly. "First outfit, coming right up." He twirled and headed toward his room with the five-pack following him.

"Walker Corrigan, if we want him to stay, you can't be rude." Norma stood with her hands on hips.

"Who says we want him to stay?" Walker groused.

Norma simply stared at him.

"Fine, it's been nice having him here." Walker rolled his eyes. "But you need to get your mind off matchmaking. He's too young, he's not my type, and you know I can't go through that. Losing Sam was too hard, and I'm not interested in that type of pain again."

"Losing Samuel was terrible and I know it hurt." Norma sat next to him and put an arm around his shoulders. "But you are young, you have so much love in your heart, and I want you to be happy."

"I *am* happy." Walker sighed. "I have friends and the ranch. My heart still hurts, but I have no plans of leaving it unprotected again."

"Sweetheart, I see the way your eyes watch Reid. Opening your heart, moving on, letting yourself love again, none of that would mean letting go of Samuel." She hugged him close. "Just maybe don't refuse the feelings, okay?"

"He's leaving. He doesn't even know I'm gay. He's clearly not interested. It's best to let things be." Walker rolled his neck. "Once he leaves, we can all get back to normal."

Reid's door opened, and the five dogs scrambled to the living room. Reid sauntered across the room, making a dramatic turn before walking back to the center.

"So, this is more of a dress-up type outfit. Maybe for a party or dance. Or maybe a meeting?"

He modeled deep red and black boots, dark wash jeans that clung to his legs, and a charcoal button-up under a deep red-fitted satin jacket with a thin black scarf tied loosely around his neck.

*Oh, shit. Do **not** think about what you could do with*

*that scarf.* Walker cleared his throat. "That's nice. Not sure you'll have much occasion to wear it here, but back in California it will be great. Didn't even know they had those types of clothes in town."

"It's all in how you put individual pieces together," Reid quipped before turning back to his room. "I won't show you *every* outfit, but number two is coming soon."

The dogs perked up and ran to follow him down the hall.

"Nice, huh?" Norma nudged Walker.

"Never said he didn't look good. That's not the issue," Walker gritted out.

Reid returned a few minutes later, dog pack in tow, in work boots, light washed jeans that fit him like a glove and looked like he'd been wearing them for years, and a muted plaid button-up with subtle western designs. "This is more for working." He did a complete one-eighty.

"Did you get a hat?" Walker demanded. "I specifically said you need a hat."

Reid pursed his lips. "Patience, cowboy." He blew a kiss to Norma and returned to his room.

The dogs followed, slower this time.

"Why you gotta snap at the boy?" Norma demanded.

"I sent him for sensible, functional clothing, and he comes back looking like he's ready to walk the damn red carpet." Walker folded both arms over his chest.

"Maybe you're just grumpy about how good he looks, and how much he's messing with that heart of yours," Norma whispered as Reid exited his room.

The dogs, panting, curled up on the rug.

"Another work outfit." Reid spun around. "These are the jeans I like best. They make my ass look fabulous."

Walker coughed. *Hell yeah, they do.*

"Okay, last outfit coming up." Reid waved.

The dogs lifted their heads, but immediately returned to sleeping.

"This next one better have a practical hat," Walker grumbled.

Reid returned wearing cuffed denim shorts, unlaced work boots flopping, a plain white t-shirt covered with a royal blue button up left unbuttoned, and a cowboy hat.

"That's the hat you picked?" Walker demanded.

"Yep," Reid popped his *p.* "Got this one, too." He switched the purposely distressed cowboy hat with a worn baseball-style cap. "Always good to have choices."

"That cowboy hat is more fashionable than functional. With the edges curled up like that, it's not going to protect you from the sun." Walker stood. "And the shorts are impractical. Your legs will get shredded by fence wire, bugs, grasses, *and* burned by the sun."

Reid, obviously nonplussed, shrugged. "Yeah, but think how great they'll look on a dance floor."

"Whatever." Walker rolled his eyes. "I'm going to go

through Jack's old hats. You need one that does what it's meant to do."

Norma sighed as Walker left the room, but not before he overheard Norma talking to Reid.

"Sorry, he's grumpy." She patted Reid's shoulder. "Fashion isn't his forte. I think you looked gorgeous. Loved all the clothes."

"Thanks." Reid smiled.

THE NEXT MORNING AT BREAKFAST, Walker entered the kitchen and tossed a large box on the counter. "Found this when I went through Jack's stuff. Didn't notice it before, thought it was just another hat. He must have set it aside, hoping you'd show up some day."

The box had *Jackson Reid Alexander* written on a sticky note and taped to the lid.

Reid brushed the dust from the top but stalled on his name. "What is it?"

"Open it," Walker commanded. "We gotta get out there, and get some work done. Hurry up."

Reid frowned, but opened the box. He gasped as he removed a charcoal gray felt cattleman style hat. A note fluttered from the brim.

*Jackson, I hope one day you'll be here to work alongside me. You'll need a hat. If you're not here before I'm gone, I still dream of seeing you on our ranch, loving it as much as*

*I do. Wear this hat with pride, and know that I loved you even if we were never allowed to meet. Love, Grandpa Jack*

"Oh, wow," Reid breathed as he slipped the hat onto his head.

"That's perfect," Norma exclaimed and clasped her hands to her chest.

"Much better." Walker nodded.

Reid took off the hat, running a hand through his hair, and then he turned the hat over and around in his hands. He smiled before hanging the hat on the back of the chair as Walker had done with his.

Breakfast was quick and quiet before they headed out the door for a full day of work.

Two weeks later, Reid found Walker in the barn office.

"Can we talk?" Reid asked from the doorway.

Walker looked up from the computer. "Sure." He shut his laptop and reached for waters from the mini refrigerator next to his desk. "What's up?"

Reid took the offered water and sat down. "I've been thinking about some things."

Walker opened his water, took a sip, and waited.

"I'm going to keep the ranch," Reid announced and then took a drink from his bottle.

Walker took a deep breath and nodded. "Staying on or just in name?"

"Haven't decided on that part yet."

"Well, I gotta say thanks first and foremost." Walker leaned forward. "You keeping the ranch means I keep a job and life I love, and all the people who choose to work here can continue. That means a lot."

Reid nodded.

"What's your thinking about staying or leaving?" Walker leaned back in his chair.

"That's the other thing I wanted to talk about." Reid scratched his head. "I feel like I've just been an observer in most of the ranch's day-to-day stuff. If I'm going to stay, I want to know what it's really like. Not just hanging around and helping here and there, I need to be completely submerged in it all so I can make an informed decision."

Walker nodded. "That can be arranged. You can continue shadowing me, but instead of observing and helping here and there, I'll have you do the majority of the work."

"No horses," Reid said quickly. "Except Cinnamon and maybe some of the other little ones."

Walker smirked, but moved on. "I think it's a great idea. I'm thrilled you want to keep the ranch, and I think making an informed decision about staying or leaving is for the best."

"Do you want me to stay?" Reid asked abruptly. *Why do I want him to want me to stay?*

Walker was quiet for a moment. "Honestly, I feel pretty neutral about the situation. I've enjoyed having you here, since you bring a nice vibe to the ranch, I think you're great for Zeke, and Norma adores you. Most importantly, I know Jack would be thrilled to have you here."

"But?" Reid hedged. *Why don't you just beg him to ask you to stay? You sound pathetic.*

"But if you leave, the ranch will go on just as it did before. I'm good at what I do. I love this ranch, it's my life. I'll make sure it continues to be the very best."

"That's one of the things that makes my decision easier. Knowing the ranch will be in good hands would make it easy to leave." *Would I stay if he asked me? Shit, yeah, I think I would.*

"So, we'll start with your submersion today?" Walker asked and checked his watch. "Almost time for lunch, so let's plan on after we eat."

"There's something else," Reid blurted.

Walker cocked a brow.

"I want to have a party." Reid's cheeks turned pink and he clasped his hands together in his lap.

"A party? Like a wiener roast or potluck?" Walker's brow furrowed. "We do that quite a bit, no problem to make it happen."

Reid pursed his lips. "I was thinking a bit bigger, fancier."

Walker raised his brows and crossed both arms on his chest. "Bigger?"

"So, I think it's important that I not only get to know the workers and families on the ranch, but some of the townsfolk, as well." Reid shifted. "I was thinking DJ, dance floor, lights, decorations, catering, the works. Give *all* the employees a break from their usual work. Tell people to dress up. Make it an event to remember."

Walker was silent.

"Thoughts?" Reid prompted.

"My first thought is it's a total waste of money. People would be just as happy with carry-in dishes and hot dogs." Walker leaned back in his chair and put both hands behind his head. "Second thought is you're definitely your Grandma Sarah's relation. I hear tell she was quite the entertainer."

"So we *can* have the party?" Reid moved to the edge of his seat.

"*You* can have the party, yes." Walker pointed at Reid.

"You'll be there, right?"

"Parties aren't really my thing. I'll help in the set up and all that. But you won't need me there for the actual event." Walker shook his head. "Norma will be thrilled to help."

"No!" Reid exclaimed. "I mean, you're like the backbone of the ranch. If you're not there, others may not come. They may think you're against it and decide it's not good for them to attend." Reid put his hands together in a praying gesture. "Please? Pretty please?" *Plus, I really want you there.*

Walker sighed deeply. "Fine. I'll be there. But I don't dance."

"Thank you! No dancing, got it." Reid smiled. "But I think dancing should be something I set as my goal to get you to do."

"I'll dance when you ride a horse," Walker drawled.

Reid narrowed his eyes. "Petty."

Walker just shrugged and laughed. "Come on, it's time for lunch."

BY THE TIME the evening meal rolled around, Reid wasn't sure he'd be able to stand from his chair once he got himself lowered down into it.

"Oh, you poor thing." Norma patted his shoulder. "After a good meal you can take a long, hot shower and you'll feel better."

"Just wait 'til morning." Walker smirked, his hair damp from the quick shower he'd already taken.

Norma swatted him with a towel.

"It's just us for dinner tonight, boys," Norma

announced as she carried a casserole dish of enchiladas to the table. "Eat up. There's chocolate cake for dessert."

Walker groaned. "This is my favorite meal." He narrowed his eyes at Norma. "What are you up to?"

Norma, hand to her bosom, gasped. "I'm appalled that you'd think I need an ulterior motive to fix your favorites."

Walker just grunted and shoveled three enchiladas onto his plate.

When the meal was finished, Reid winced as he pushed himself from the table. "Can I save my chocolate cake until after I shower?"

"Of course, sugar." Norma waved him away from the table. "Big glass of cold milk or piping hot coffee will be here waiting along with your cake when you're done."

Reid stiffly limped from the room and down the hall. The duck dogs followed.

"What are you up to?" Walker demanded.

"Moi?" Norma batted her lashes.

Walker waited.

"Child, I've loved you like my own since the day you came here. My heart broke for you when you lost Samuel, and I swore I'd do everything in my power to bring love to your heart again." Norma's eyes welled with tears.

Walker leaned forward on his elbows, face in hands.

"I love you, too. But you don't need to play matchmaker. He's not interested."

"Pishaw," Norma groused. "If that's the only excuse you're still holding onto you better prepare to let it go."

"No, I mean, that's just one of the reasons...," Walker sputtered. "He's young, he doesn't know if he's staying, and I can't go through losing someone again. Plus, what about Samuel?"

"What about him?" Norma patted Walker's hand. "That man loved you as much as you loved him. But, baby, he's gone. Samuel would want you happy, just like I know you'd want him happy if he'd been the one left behind."

"Even if you take the Samuel piece out of the equation, too much still doesn't add up." Walker pinched the bridge of his nose.

"Well, now, I never was too good in math, so pardon me while I ignore your equations and adding." Norma stood and started the coffee pot. "What I know are the facts. Fact: You've smiled more and been more alive since Reid came around. Fact: That man brings a sparkle to this ranch that's been missing for forever. Fact: He is interested. Look at you, how could he not be? But he's being respectful. He's got so much going on, I doubt he's even given one single moment to thinking about your sexuality. Fact: You're thirty-two. He's twenty-seven. That is *not* too much of an age gap. Hell, child, my Benny was seventeen years my senior and we lived a long and happy life together. Fact: He may not have made his decision completely, but he's already said he'll keep the ranch. You need to give him reason to stay." Norma paused her fact spewing and stood with her hands on hips.

"What if I'm not enough reason for him to stay?" Walker mumbled.

Norma walked over and pulled him into a hug. "I don't see how that could be, but if you're not reason enough then I'll eat my words and pack his suitcase for him."

"I'm scared." Walker spoke softly with his head against Norma's waist.

"I know you are, but that's okay. Feeling scared means you're *feeling* and that's a good thing." Norma leaned down and kissed the top of his head. "Now, you're going to take the liniment rub in there and offer to help him with his sore muscles."

"That's the cheesiest thing I've ever heard." Walker scoffed.

"He needs to know where you stand if we're going to move this thing along." Norma released Walker and moved to pour her coffee. "Liniment is in the medicine cabinet. Cake will be on the counter. I'm going to take a nice long bath and read in my room for the rest of the night."

Walker watched her leave. "I can't do this," he whispered to himself.

"Yes, you can," Norma shot back before disappearing to the opposite wing of the house.

Walker took a deep shuddering breath and headed for the medicine cabinet.

He stood outside Reid's door for what seemed like ages.

Was he ready for this?

Could he even do this?

What exactly was *this*?

He knocked lightly even though he could still hear the shower running. Cracking the door slightly, he peeked into the room. All five dogs lifted their heads and scampered to greet him. Louise yipped and immediately the shower shut off.

Walker's heart pounded as he stood awkwardly in the middle of Reid's room with the tin of liniment balm in his hands.

Reid, hair dripping, stuck his head out from the bathroom door. "What's up?"

"Oh, um, sorry to barge in," Walker stammered. "It's just, uh, Norma said I should bring you this liniment since you're so sore."

Reid ducked back into the bathroom for a moment before returning, wearing a tank and cut-off sweat shorts and rubbing a towel through his hair. "Liniment?" Reid wrinkled his nose. "What's that?"

"It's good for sore muscles. Doesn't smell too great, but you rub it on and it helps relieve stiffness and soreness." Walker held up the tin. "If you want, I can get your back and calves and then you can get the rest of whatever hurts."

Reid narrowed his eyes but shrugged and pulled the tank over his head before easing himself face first onto the bed. "The shower really did help, but I hurt all over. Tomorrow is gonna suck." His words were muffled into the pillow.

Walker's jaw clenched and his heart stuttered as he took in the perfect form on the bed before him. He unscrewed the tin and scooped out some of the balm. Closing his eyes and taking a deep breath, Walker gently touched his hand to Reid's lower leg and began to rub.

"Ah, God, that hurts, but like it feels so good, too." Reid moaned into the pillow.

Walker moved to the foot of the bed and scooped more liniment from the tin. Using both hands, he massaged the balm into Reid's calves as Reid groaned beneath his touch.

*Holy shit, I'm not going to make it through this.* Walker he gritted his teeth and finished Reid's lower legs and moved to the side of the bed to rub the liniment into Reid's back and shoulders. *Probably be too much to straddle him, huh?* Walker snickered to himself at the thought.

Reid turned his head on the pillow which brought his gaze and attention almost directly to Walker's less than subtle hard-on behind his lounge pants. Reid's eyes widened before he rolled to his side and gingerly lifted himself from the bed and stood to face Walker.

Reid's nostrils flared, and he cleared his throat before speaking. "Listen, you're hot and I'd climb you like a tree, but I don't get involved with straight guys. I'm not an experiment or someone's secret to keep on the downlow."

Walker blinked rapidly, until his brain finally signaled him to speak. "You think I'm hot?"

Reid scoffed. "Have you looked in the mirror? You're a walkin' wet dream in a cowboy hat and boots." Reid winced. "But like I said—"

"I'm flattered you think I'm hot, the feeling is mutual. For the record, maybe you should have your sensors checked, because I'd be more than happy to have you climb me any which way, and I'd most definitely be inclined to return the favor."

"Wait, what?" Reid frowned and took a step back. "You're gay?"

"Most definitely."

"Are you sure?" Reid continued to frown.

"Why do I feel like I'm back explaining to my parents that this isn't just a phase?" Walker groused.

"I'm sorry. That was a stupid question. Of course you're sure," Reid mumbled. "I'm just surprised is all."

Walker waited.

"I guess I've had a lot on my mind and it didn't even

dawn on me that you're gay. Maybe I was too focused on Zeke? I don't know, but I'm sorry I didn't know, and I'm sorry I'm acting dumb." Reid blushed.

"You're gorgeous," Walker blurted and his eyes went wide. "Sorry, I'm so very out of practice with this."

Reid grabbed his tank and slid it on before sitting on the side of the bed. "It's okay. Go slow." He patted the bed, inviting Walker to sit.

"I like you. And I've been arguing with my head and heart ever since you showed up."

"What are they saying?" Reid whispered.

"My head says you're too young, you're not my type, you're not even staying, and I don't do relationships." Walker sighed as he sat beside Reid.

"And your heart?" Reid bumped against Walker's shoulder.

"My heart says it's been way too long since I've felt this way and maybe I should take a chance." Walker leaned back on his hands.

"So? Which are you siding with?"

"When I lost Samuel," Walker started but stopped when Reid gasped.

"Were they the father and son who died in the drunk driving accident?"

Walker nodded. "Losing Samuel was devastating. I swore I'd never let myself be that way with anyone else, that way I'd never hurt like that again."

Reid nodded and placed a hand over Walker's.

"But then you showed up, and try as I might, I can't stop feeling drawn to you and happy to have you around. I find myself making excuses just to be in the same area as you." Walker chuckled. "All those chores today? Any other new person on the ranch would have been assigned to any number of the hands to teach them. But you? I didn't even give it a second thought, I wanted to be the one teaching you and watching you and spending time with you."

"Wow, I'm flattered," Reid said.

"Part of me wants to lock up my heart and never let it out again, keep it safe from you and whatever this might be." Walker waved a hand between them.

"And the other part?"

"The other part says it's about time I allow myself to feel something again, allow myself to be happy again." Walker turned toward Reid. "Maybe you don't feel the same way. Maybe you do and I'll be terrible at this. Maybe you'll leave and I'll be destroyed. Maybe—"

Reid held a finger to Walker's lips and hushed him. "Maybe you should just kiss me."

Walker's eyes flashed. "Maybe that's the best thing I've heard all day."

He leaned in.

Reid moved forward slightly, his gaze on Walkers lips until the very last moment.

Reid closed his eyes and let Walker's mouth overtake his own. Walker's lips were silky soft against Reid's, but there was no question who was leading.

Walker's hand came up to hold the back of Reid's head and deepen the kiss. When Walker's tongue touched Reid's lip, Reid opened for him and groaned as their tongues met and mated.

One of the ducks barked.

Walker and Reid pulled apart, both breathing heavily and smiling.

Reid bit his lip and blushed. "I guess they're tired of being stuck in here."

"Probably," Walker agreed. He stood and pulled Reid to stand next to him. "Was that okay?"

Reid nodded and trailed a kiss along Walker's jawline until he reached Walker's mouth where he whispered, "That was more than okay, and I hope we can do it again and again."

"Deal." Walker chuckled and wrapped Reid in his arms. "How about that chocolate cake?"

"Perfect."

## 10

"*A*re you sure you don't want to just have a bonfire and roast some hotdogs?" Walker grumped as he ducked to keep from getting knocked in the head by the large board Reid carried to the dance floor's construction area.

"Oh, I want a bonfire and hotdogs, but a party isn't a party without a dance floor, lights, and music. You have to set the atmosphere." Reid grinned and placed the board down with the others. His arms and legs would have been an aching mass of goo a week or so ago, but each day of doing chores with Walker and the other employees had built up his muscles even more than dancing ever did.

Walker laughed and rolled his eyes. "Fine, let's build some atmosphere."

While the two men built a wooden base and floor

along with four corner posts and connecting boards where lights would hang, they chatted.

"How old were you when you came out?" Reid held a board for Walker to nail.

"Probably about thirteen?" Walker held one nail in his teeth as he swiftly pounded the other one into the board with the hammer.

"Pretty young." Reid gave a low whistle. "How'd your parents take it?"

Walker stopped working for a moment and adjusted his hat. "That's probably why I was able to figure things out so young and come out with no issues, my parents were gone. Never knew my dad, but my grandma always said I wasn't missing out on anything. My mom ran off to Hollywood with some wannabe movie producer when I was two. Never saw her again. Grandma told me when I was much older that Mom had followed that guy straight into drugs and prostitution all while believing she would eventually be a big star. She overdosed on heroin when I was about eight, I think. I didn't know any of this until I was an adult."

"Wow, that's a lot. I'm sorry for all that awfulness. So, your grandma was pretty great, huh?" Reid went back to holding the board as Walker returned to his task.

"The greatest. I'm likely bias, but she was always there, always supportive. She had my mom pretty young, so she wasn't an older grandma. She was in her thirties when I was born." Walker removed his hat and scratched his head.

"Were you nervous to tell her you were gay?"

"Not really. We had a great relationship, and I never feared she wouldn't support me. When I told her, she just smiled and gave me a hug. She never made a big deal about girls to me before, so maybe she knew or suspected? But after I told her, she would point out cute guys all the time on movies and television and in magazines."

"That sounds really nice. Sounds like you had a good friend in her."

"Oh, I wouldn't call her my friend. She made it clear from the very beginning that she was my parent figure and that there were rules and expectations and conse-quences. But she was supportive and helpful and loving along the way." Walker chuckled.

"Do you still get to see her?"

"She's got a tiny little apartment a few towns over, and I try to go see her every other week or so." Walker hefted another board from the pile and placed it on the foundation. "I'd really like to move her here. She's getting to a point where living on her own is just starting to get hard, and I *know* she's not going to want to go to an assisted living facility. I think living on the ranch would be good for her. Plus, she really loves it here. Part of me thinks she'd like to ask to move here but thinks she'd be a bother." Walker positioned the board so it was lined up and waited for Reid to hold it in place before securing it with two nails. "Honestly, I think it would be great for Grandma and Norma and the kids to have her here."

"You should ask her." Reid shrugged. "Can't hurt."

"You're right. Maybe next time I go visit." Walker glanced at Reid, his eyes aglow. "Maybe you could go with me."

Reid smirked. "Maybe."

"What about you? When did you come out?" Walker stood after attaching the last board to the frame and walked to the cooler. He grabbed two waters and tossed one to Reid before opening his own and taking a long swig.

Reid grimaced. "Well, I probably knew I was gay from about age ten. I hadn't named it, but I knew I was different." He opened his water and took a drink. "I didn't finally admit to myself I was gay until about fifteen. And I didn't come out until I was in college."

"Because you knew your parents wouldn't be supportive?"

Reid walked over to Bert and hopped up to sit on the tailgate. "You need some background on Father Jack because he's very unlike Grandpa Jack."

Walker joined Reid on the truck's tailgate.

"My father pretty much wanted nothing to do with me until I was old enough to possibly be his little protégé. By that time, he was a complete stranger, and I didn't want to be around him. He tried forcing me to go to the office with him, but I begged my mom to not make me. Jack got angry and decided I wasn't worthy of his teaching and guidance and told me to never ask him for business advice or assistance."

"Sounds like a prick." Walker swung his legs from the truck.

"Complete and total prick." Reid nodded. "I always wondered how my mom ended up with him because she was pretty cool. I asked her when I was older. Said she fell for his charm when she was very young and naïve. I told her she should leave him. She shrugged and said she never really saw him so she didn't have to deal with him much. And the money she had access to because of him was being used to fund charities and non-profits and scholarships. She said she had no interest in marrying again, had tons of friends, a happy life, and staying married to him allowed her funds to do what she loved most which is helping others."

"That's sort of awesome and sort of sad all at the same time, ya know?"

"Agreed." Reid took another drink. "I told my mom I was gay the summer after freshman year of college. She was pretty great. Said she loved me no matter what and then went on to make several large donations to PFLAG and GLAAD and some local LGBTQ organizations." Reid chuckled. "Jack would have died to know where that money was going, but it was hers to do with what she wanted and he never checked."

"I take it Father Jack wasn't as accepting?" Walker shifted again so his shoulder and thigh were in contact with Reid's.

"Understatement." Reid leaned into Walker. "It was a whole year after I told my mom before I told Jack. I didn't plan on it, but he happened to be home and was going on and on about something in the news regarding the LGBTQ community and I just sat listening to him with this ball of anger and sadness growing in me until I felt like I couldn't breathe. I don't even remember the exact words that made me snap, but he'd been spewing such hateful words that I finally blew up."

"What did you say?"

"I screamed, 'Shut up!' and when he looked at me as if I'd grown three heads, so I said, 'I'm gay, Dad.'" Reid leaned more heavily into Walker. "He laughed at first as if I was telling a joke. I tried to calm myself and told him again, 'I'm gay. Always have been, always will be.'"

"What did he do?"

"His face turned so red I seriously thought he was going to have a stroke. He screamed and hollered and slammed things all while saying no son of his was going to embarrass his good name by being a faggot. I watched as he threw his fit and when his tirade finally came to a slowing point, he slumped down in a chair."

"Was your mom there?"

"No, she was at a charity event. I don't even know how Dad and I ended up in the house at the same time as that almost never happened. But once he sat down, he sputtered nonsense about it being a phase, how I'd grow out of it, how I'd come around, and I just needed to find the right girl." Reid snorted.

"What did you do?"

"I stood up, leaned my hands on the table and said, 'Dad, I'm gay. The *right* girl will be a guy. Sorry. I take dick in the ass and enjoy it. Immensely.' The look on his face was priceless. Like he wasn't sure if he wanted to kill me or barf. I left the room before he could decide to do either. Had almost zero contact with him from that point on, which was perfect, until the reading of the will after Grandpa Jack died."

Walker threw his head back and laughed. "You did not say that, seriously?"

Reid joined the laughter. "I did. I mean, it was crude, but he needed to hear it."

Walker put his arm behind Reid on the truck bed and leaned in close. "I guess that answers the question of top or bottom."

Reid laughed. "Oh, there's never been a question. I can be vers if needed, but I'm a bottom boy at heart."

"Good to know," Walker whispered in Reid's ear before trailing a kiss along his jaw.

Reid moaned and lifted his head to allow Walker access to his neck. When Walker's hand gripped Reid's thigh and moved higher, Reid pulled back abruptly. "Wait, we're in broad daylight. Does everyone know you're gay?"

"Mostly." Walker nodded. "Many of the people here at the ranch were here before I came. Jack never made a big deal over my sexuality. When Samuel and I started dating, I knew there were two guys who weren't okay with it. One left and Jack fired the other because of his treatment of Samuel and me. It's never really been a problem."

Reid smiled and leaned back into Walker's space. "Mmm, that works perfectly. Everyone knows you're gay, everyone knows I'm gay."

"Well, don't most straight people think the gay guys they know should automatically hook up and fall in love?" Walker teased and nuzzled against Reid's neck before freezing and pulling back quickly. "I mean, like dating, I don't mean fall in *love* love," he stammered.

Reid laughed. "No worries. I knew what you meant." He kissed at the corner of Walker's mouth. "And of course two gay guys on a ranch are required to be attracted to each other and get together."

"Maybe you should think about Ezekiel? Is he more your type?" Walker was the one to pull back this time.

"What?" Reid chuckled. "First, he's *way* too young. Second, he's like a baby gay who hasn't even discovered himself yet." Reid began kissing Walker again and didn't stop even as he spoke again. "And I'm not interested in corrupting the youngin' with a threesome."

Walker laughed against Reid's lips. "Agreed."

Reid deepened the kiss.

Walker let himself enjoy the kiss for a few moments before pulling back. "We need to keep working if this fancy dance floor is going to get finished."

"Okay, okay," Reid whined but smiled and hopped off the truck. "Let's get busy."

THE DAY of the party dawned sunny and absolutely perfect. Not too hot. Not too cold.

Walker bumped Reid's hip as they entered the kitchen. The two had shared many kisses and soft touches recently. *I tried not to develop feelings, damn it, I really tried. But now I'm stuck between wanting more and being scared to death he'll rip my heart to shreds if he leaves.* Walker's hand brushed against Reid's before taking it in his own. Reid returned the gesture with a squeeze and light caress.

"Caterers will be here around three o'clock to start setting up and cooking," Norma checked off something on a list. "I can't believe you didn't want me to cook."

"Reid wanted you to have the day and night off cooking duties." Walker put an arm around her shoulders.

"You deserve a break! We've got dancing to do," Reid crowed. "The DJ will be here at five o'clock to get his area ready."

"All the ranch employees are attending, and the few townspeople you invited are coming, as well." Walker flipped through his phone as he checked the RSVP's.

"I still feel bad that I couldn't invite the whole town." Reid pouted.

"Sugar, stop." Norma patted his shoulder. "You can invite more next time."

Reid beamed. "Hear that? Norma has given permission for a next time because she already knows it's going to be the best party this ranch has ever seen."

"Norma, don't fill his head. You'll create a monster," Walker groused but pulled Reid into a hug and kissed him. "I'm sure the party is going to be fabulous."

he party *was* fabulous.

Walker had a hard time keeping his eyes off Reid as the party went on. Reid's face had been filled with a huge smile from the moment the first guests started to arrive, and he hadn't stopped smiling as he visited with ranch families and the visitors from in town.

Walker made note to ask Reid just what Doctor Phips had said to him that had him throwing his head back in laughter and shooting a warm smiled Walker's way.

The food was beyond delicious, and Walker enjoyed seeing Norma able to just visit and have fun. Although, he could tell she was a bit bent as people raved about food that wasn't made by her. The DJ played a wide variety of songs that allowed everyone, young and old and in between, to enjoy the music and dancing. Reid's suggestion of lighting gave the absolute perfect atmosphere to the dance floor and surrounding area.

But the highlight of Walker's night was watching Reid teach eager party-goers how to dance. Nothing brought people to the dance floor like a good group line dance, and Reid proved that to be true as he taught the steps to *Cupid Shuffle* and *Wobble*. The more adventurous dancers stayed on the floor to glean dance moves from Reid as other songs played. Reid was happy, patient, and made every single person on the dance floor feel special. Walker's chest was warm and his smile bright as he watched Reid in his element.

When Reid walked over to the DJ and made a request, Walker narrowed his eyes in curiosity. But then a slow song started playing and Walker knew what Reid was up to. He watched as Reid pulled ranch hands and their wives to the floor. Youngsters, not ready to be off the stage, swayed to the slower beat in a cute way that only kids can pull off. Norma laughed as Dr. Phips pulled her to the floor, and they began a classic box-step in keeping with the tune.

"May I have this dance?" Reid tapped Walker on the shoulder.

"I told you, I don't dance," Walker grumbled.

"It's painless, I promise." Reid clasped his hands in front of him. "This is me begging. *Please* dance with me? I at least went *near* a horse. That has the earn me at least a little something."

Walker rolled his eyes but grinned and stepped to the dance floor with Reid. They mimicked the box-step Norma and the doctor were enjoying.

"Perfect party," Walker stated as he squeezed Reid's hand in his own.

"Yeah, it really did turn out amazingly well." Reid nodded as his fingers toyed at the back of Walker's neck.

"What did Doc Phips say that had you laughing so hard?"

"The first time I met her, she was all cryptic and shit about how I should keep my mind and my heart open, how I'd be good for the ranch and the ranch would be good for me."

Walker cocked a brow and waited.

"So tonight she told me I looked good, and she could tell the ranch was doing wonders for me. She added she'd never seen you looking so happy." Reid shrugged but smirked. "She said a little bird had told her that perhaps we were good for each other. And then she told me to never question her fortune telling skills again."

Walker laughed. "Doc is something else, for sure."

Reid sobered for a moment. "Do you think it's weird that we're together?"

"How's that?"

"I mean, you're beyond attractive, and I enjoy spending time with you," Reid began.

"Same, so what's the issue?" Walker pressed.

"Would we have found each other attractive and

enjoyable if we'd met in a city full of a thousand gay men? Or are we just settling because we're the only choices?" Reid worried his lip between his teeth.

Walker was quiet for a bit.

Another slow song came on. Some couples exchanged partners. Reid and Walker stayed together.

"I think, no. I *know* I'd find you attractive no matter where I see you." Walker stroked Reid's knuckles with his thumb. "I swore I'd never get in another relationship after losing Samuel, but then you came along. I fought it, but finally admitted I couldn't fight it any longer and really didn't even want to. But if you feel like you're just settling for me, I can understand and respect that."

Reid gasped. "No, that's not at all what I meant." He glanced around the dance floor. "Can we go somewhere more private?"

Walker led Reid from the floor, and they made their way up to the small incline to the dark side of the house. "Better?"

Reid nodded. "I didn't mean I was settling for you." He sighed. "I overheard some people talking about how quickly we became an item, and how you were probably thrilled I showed up so you'd have someone to fuck."

Walker's rage was palpable even in the dark. "Who the hell said that?"

"Honestly, I don't know who they were. The voices were behind me while I was talking to the caterer; they must not have realized I was standing so close. By the time I turned around, there was a large group of people and no way to tell who had spoken." Reid sighed. "It's really not important *who* said it, as long as it's not true."

"First, you'd been here a fairly long time before we were anything more than friends." Walker cupped Reid's cheek. "Second, it's no one's damn business. Third, I wasn't pining for someone to fuck. You just snuck your way into my heart. Fourth," Walker kissed at the corner of Reid's mouth, "I have no plans to *just* fuck you." He captured Reid's lips in a warm kiss that quickly became hot, fiery, and passionate.

Reid moaned, wrapped his arms around Walker's neck, and returned the kiss with everything he had.

Walker maneuvered Reid toward the house and pressed him against the wall. He took hold of Reid's hips. Walker's kisses stuttered when their jean-clad cocks met and rubbed together.

"It would be wrong to leave my own party, right?" Reid panted against Walker's ear as the two thrust their hips.

Walker gripped Reid's ass and picked him up.

Reid wrapped his legs around Walker's waist.

"Yeah, probably wouldn't be the best move for the host." Walker rocked his cock hard into Reid's. "But we can always make sure to pick up right where we are *after* the party."

Reid whimpered as Walker nipped at his collarbone. "Promise?"

"Definitely," Walker growled attacking Reid's lips with a hungry, wet kiss.

The moment was interrupted as the night filled with the sounds of explosions.

"What the fuck is that?" Walker released Reid and the two men ran toward the party.

The sound of frightened horses neighing and kicking in the barn caught their attention.

"Shit, you go to the party, see what happened. I'll go check on the horses." Walker let go of Reid's hand and sprinted toward the barn just as several ranch hands ran toward the barn, as well.

Reid reached the party, breathless and concerned. "What happened?"

"Fire crackers," someone said. "Some kids from town must have made their way out here and set off some Black Cats as their way of having fun."

"Dr. Phips tried to catch them, but they ran off before she could see their faces. They were right beside the barn, spooked the horses a lot more than it spooked the people I'm afraid." Norma frowned and held a hand to her chest. "I pray those horses stay put. A spooked horse is an injury waiting to happen."

"Injury to the horse or the people?" Reid asked, fear furrowing his brow.

"Both." Norma grimaced.

Wes came running from the barn. "Two of the horses have some cuts and scrapes from thrashing in their pens. But the newest one was too scared and too strong, she busted through her pen and jumped the fence. She's on the run and possibly injured. Walker went after her. Three others are riding with him. I need all hands on deck to help with the injured horses and calm down the others."

Reid watched helplessly as many went to offer assistance. "I don't know what to do. I want to help, but I can't go near them, especially if they're worked up." He ran his fingers through his hair and clasped his hands at the base of his neck.

"Don't you worry about it," Norma cooed as she rubbed his back. "We'll stay here and help with tear down and clean up."

Reid attempted to stay busy with Norma and the others while supplies and food were cleaned, gathered, and packed. Finally, he could take it no more.

"Think it's okay to at least go check on Cinnamon?" Reid shuffled his feet and shot a worried glance at the barn.

"I'm sure that baby girl would be thrilled to see you," Norma patted his shoulder, "but you gotta remember most of the other horses are in there, and they had a bit of excitement tonight. They may be a little worked up."

Reid nodded and pulled at his ear. "Maybe I'll just go down and ask if Cinnamon is okay."

"You do what feels best, baby." Norma rubbed a hand between Reid's shoulders.

*You can do this.*

*The horses are likely more afraid than you.*

*You can do this.*

*Cinnamon is probably scared. She'd love a friendly face.*

*You can do this.*

*None of those horses would purposely hurt you.*

*You can do this.*

*It's not like you're getting in the pen with the big horses.*

*You can do this.*

*If it's crazy or seems dangerous in the barn, you can leave.*

*You can do this.*

Reid attempted to build his courage with each step toward the barn.

When he opened the small side door to the barn, he was greeted with the earthy aroma of hay, straw, feed, and horse. He took a deep breath and felt a wave of calm rush over him. He wrinkled his nose. Since when had the nasty smell of the ranch and the barn become something he *welcomed*?

Instead of turning right toward the office, Reid moved farther down the hallway and took a left to the main barn. Nickering, neighing, and various other horse sounds mixed with the quiet chatter of the men working on the horses.

Reid saw Wes and raised a hand. "Think Cinnamon could use a visitor?" he called softly.

Wes gave him a thumbs up.

Reid walked toward Cinnamon's stall with light feet and peeked around the door to her pen.

The nicker that greeted him was music to Reid's ears. "Hey, girl, how are you?" He slid open the door to her pen and entered.

Cinnamon nudged his chest and leaned against him.

"Scary night, huh?" Reid scratched her face and let her nuzzle against his hand. "Sorry, baby, I should have brought a treat. Next time, huh?"

Reid spent the next thirty minutes comforting Cinnamon.

When the sound of pounding hooves echoed through the night, Reid and Cinnamon both perked their ears.

"Wes, let's get her walked for about fifteen minutes. She's hot; get her some water and hose her down. We'll have some hay ready for her once she's cool," Walker's voice rumbled through the barn.

Wes turned over what he was working on to another hand and took Zeke with him to work on the runaway horse.

Reid gave Cinnamon a last bit of love and left her stall to find Walker. With all of his focus on finding

Walker, Reid paid very little attention to the other horses around him.

"Hey, is she okay?" Reid asked as he found Walker at the edge of the corral where Wes and Zeke were walking the biggest, blackest, fiercest-looking horse Reid had ever seen.

"Yeah, she just got majorly spooked."

"What's her name?" Reid asked.

"Beauty," Walker replied before pulling Reid into a hug. "You okay? Sorry I had to rush off like that."

"Yeah, I'm good. I was worried about you both." Reid's words were muffled into Walker's shirt.

"Must have been super worried if it brought you to the barn voluntarily," Walker teased before moving to lean against the corral fence.

"I came to see Cinnamon, because I didn't want her to be alone." Reid shrugged and leaned against the fence next to Walker. "Must have been the adrenaline of fear, but the usual nasty-ass stench of the barn actually calmed me when I walked in. How weird is that?"

Walker chuckled. "Told ya this place would grow on you." He bumped his shoulder against Reid's.

"How far did Beauty get?" Reid watched Wes and Zeke lead the majestic creature in slower and slower laps while she cooled down.

"Remember that fence we fixed a while back? She had begun to slow up when we caught up to her. We got her slowed enough to turn her around and bring her back in." Walker repositioned his hat. "But she's hot and it's not safe or humane to put a hot horse up without cooling her down."

"I thought I'd heard it was dangerous to use cold water, let them drink or eat, when they are hot?"

"Myths. Best to walk them first, but cold water is fine to hose them with. Since the evening isn't super warm, the hose water will likely be lukewarm." Walker reached across his body to touch Reid's arm propped on the fence. "Probably best to have her drink cool water rather than cold, but only because they usually drink more when the water isn't super cold."

"She's massive," Reid murmured.

"She's one of the most gorgeous animals I've ever seen." Walker squeezed Reid's elbow. "We've not had her long. She's got a lot of fear and bad habits, but we'll get her straightened out."

"She looks angry and mean." Reid shivered.

"Nah, she's just not had the right upbringing. No love." Walker stared at the horse. "You'll be amazed at her transformation. You won't even recognize her when we're done with her."

"I'll take your word for it," Reid said. "Or I'll watch her transformation from afar."

Wes led Beauty to the barn. "I'll finish her up, boss," Wes waved to Walker.

Walker and Reid moved around the barn, checking

the stalls and horses. Reid stayed more in the middle, farther away from the animals.

"Gotta say I'm pretty impressed you're even in the barn," Walker bumped Reid's shoulder as they neared Cinnamon's stall.

Reid shrugged. "Guess all the worry overrode my fear. At least for tonight."

"Maybe you can use this as proof that the horses aren't out to maim and maul you. Spend some more time here," Walker suggested.

Reid gave a noncommittal grunt.

AFTER A LATE-NIGHT SHOWER, Reid made his way to the kitchen and found Walker leaning against the sink looking out the window.

"You okay?" Reid lay a hand on Walker's bare shoulder.

Walker shuddered as if to clear his mind before turning to take Reid in his arms. "Yeah, just a lot on my mind."

"Beauty?"

"Well, yes, she could have been injured or killed. I want to make sure the kids who did this know how dangerous it was, as well." Walker paused.

"But? It sounds like there's something else." Reid pulled back and looked directly into Walker's eyes.

"It's probably nothing," Walker began.

"Go on," Reid encouraged.

"Pine Ridge sits on a geothermal pocket. It's not the biggest around by any means, but it's large enough to net a substantial profit for the geothermal company who purchases it."

"Okay?" Reid scowled. "Are you saying you want to dig up the ranch? Sell to someone? I'm confused."

"No, not at all." Walker shook his head and moved to sit on the counter top. "When I first came here, multiple geothermal companies were pursuing Jack and trying to buy the ranch or at least part of it so they'd have access to the pocket."

"Was Jack interested in this?"

"Not at all. He told them in no uncertain terms that no part of his ranch was for sale and it *never* would be." Walker drummed his fingers on the counter.

"So what's the problem?" Reid moved to stand between Walker's legs.

"Like I said, probably nothing. But the biggest of the companies contacted me this morning suggesting a large purchase price and asking for a meeting." Walker draped his arms around Reid's neck.

"So tell them no," Reid replied.

"The issue is that the company made mention of a *new party* involved in their pursuit of the ranch, and made a point to bring up that the new party has informed them that the ranch may not be in a stable ownership position at this point." Walker massaged Reid's neck.

Reid scowled. And then his eyes widened. "My dad?"

Walker shrugged. "I don't know. Maybe? It would make sense."

"But why? What would my dad have to do with any of it?" Reid wondered aloud.

"Maybe he has a hand in the company? Owns shares? Wants to mess with the ranch so that you sell and move on?" Walker shrugged. "There's any number of reasons."

"What are you going to do?"

"I think you and I will pay a visit to my grandma and have a meeting with the company next week." Walker tipped up Reid's chin to kiss him. "We'll do the meeting one day, spend the night, and visit Grandma the next day. Plan?"

"I like it." Reid kissed Walker. "I'm worried about whatever this meeting could bring about. But I'm happy to meet Grandma...," Reid paused, "Corrigan?"

"Yeah, my mom was never married so she kept her maiden name." Walker trailed his hands down Reid's back and gripped his waist, pulling him closer before kissing him deeply. "And we don't *have* to hold off on anything while we're here. We're in a pretty quiet wing of the house, but an overnight at the hotel could be a fun night, ya know?"

Reid reached up and wrapped his arms around Walker's neck and returned the kisses before murmuring, "Mmm, I think that sounds like a very fun night." He pulled back a bit. "I'm fine with what we've got going, not too fast, not too slow, but I'm not against going farther."

Walker groaned. "Same. I didn't want to rush into anything, but I'm definitely on board with moving things along." He hugged Reid close and sighed. "Probably better hit the hay." He kissed the tip of Reid's nose and ran fingers through the hair at the base of Reid's neck. "I gave all the guys an extra two hours of sleep in the morning, so I have to be sure I'm up and ready to do the work."

"Aww, that was nice, but why? Doesn't that just leave you with extra? And even less sleep?" Reid pouted as he defended Walker.

"I'm the one in charge. Those men worked hard tonight. They deserve it. I don't mind, and the head man has to be ready to shoulder the work. The ranch is only as good as those in charge lead it to be." Walker kissed Reid then pushed him away as he hopped from the counter. "Sleep tight."

## 12

"Good morning," Reid mumbled as he poured coffee.

Walker stopped mid-sip of coffee. "Why are you up? I didn't mean you had to help. Go on back to bed." He walked to the counter and pulled Reid into an embrace. Walker nuzzled Reid's neck and kissed along his jawline. "Although, I can't say I won't enjoy this for just a bit before heading out to the barn."

Reid tipped back his head, offering Walker more of his neck, and rocked his hips into Walker's. "Mmm, I'll get up early every day if this is how you greet me."

Walker chuckled. "Seriously, I didn't expect you to help. Go on back to bed for a while."

"The ranch is only as good as those in charge lead it to be," Reid recited Walker's words from the night before.

Walker's eyes sparkled and his face softened into a warm smile. "I like the sound of that. Working alongside you today sounds perfect." He tipped Reid's chin and kissed him. "Let's see if we can wrangle up something to eat."

"There are leftovers from the party." Reid went to work gathering and plating food. "Your breakfast is served, sir."

They sat adjacently at the table, their knees nudging and teasing.

"I want to learn to ride," Reid blurted.

Walker's fork clattered against his plate. "Say what?"

Reid shrugged. "I felt helpless last night when I couldn't help with Beauty and the other horses. If I'm going to live on a ranch, I can't avoid horses forever."

"Are you *sure?*" Walker cocked his head. "There are tons of things you can do here without having to ride horses."

"Yes, I'm sure." Reid shivered. "I'm scared, but it's important to me. I can't be part of this place if I can't get close to the main reason this ranch exists. My grandfather was a horse man, so it's got to be *somewhere* in my blood."

Walker beamed. "Great. We'll start slow. Get you comfortable just being around the horses first. Then we'll figure out which would be best for you to ride." He winked and waggled his brows.

Reid groaned and bit his lip. "I know exactly what would be best for me to ride."

It was Walker's turn to groan.

"Come here, baby. I've got some sugar for you." Walker's voice echoed softly among the horse's noises in the barn.

"That sounds promising," Reid murmured at Walker's side.

Walker laughed and dug into his pocket to produce sugar cubes. "I meant for the horse, you goof." He leaned over and kissed Reid. "But I promise to give you some sugar later."

Reid sighed. "I'll hold you to that." He moved back suddenly and tensed. "So, this is my girl, huh? She's a shit ton bigger than Cinnamon."

"Well, Cinnamon isn't old enough to ride, so the next best horse is Buttercup." Walker held out a sugar cube, and the mare gobbled it up before nuzzling her nose against Walker's chest. "Buttercup is a total sweetie." Walker offered her another sugar cube. "She likes sugar cubes, but the true way to her heart is with carrots. Head over to the fridge and grab a couple. She'll love you forever if you give her a carrot."

Reid took a deep breath. "Love me forever or eat me along with the carrot."

Walker chuckled. "Damn, man, when was the last time you heard of a horse *eating* a person?"

Reid shrugged and turned for the fridge across the barn. "Could happen," he grumbled. "Maybe."

"Horses don't eat meat. Some are known to be biters, but Buttercup has never had that issue." Walker brushed the horse as Reid returned with three large carrots.

"What's she here for? Don't all the horses have some sort of problem you're trying to fix?" Reid stood a couple arm's lengths from Buttercup's stall.

"Nah, some are here for breaking, some for training, some for rehabilitation. Buttercup was just a purchase Jack made. She's not a racer, but she's a smooth ride and a good horse. We can trust her. She's not easily spooked. I take her out to ride the fence sometimes. No attitude, no trouble, great gal." Walker connected a lead to Buttercup's bridle. "Come on, we'll go out in the corral. The arena is being used for training right now, but the corral is open."

"Am I *riding* today?" Reid had stepped back and allowed Walker to lead the horse past, but stood stock still as he asked his question.

"Not unless you think you want to," Walker hollered back.

Reid scoffed and kicked at the dirt before following. When he reached the corral, he stood by the fence and watched Walker lead Buttercup around once.

"Okay, bring her a carrot. It's your turn." Walker waved Reid over.

Reid handed Walker two carrots and kept one in his hand.

"Hold it out to her." Walker demonstrated. "If it's small, hold it flat in your hand so her teeth don't nip, but the carrot is long enough she can take a bite from it first."

Reid did as instructed, wincing as he offered the carrot to Buttercup. When he didn't lose a finger, he chuckled and watched as the horse gobbled up the carrot. "Dang, she eats that like I eat cake."

Walker bumped Reid's shoulder. "Now, hold the rest of it in your hand, but keep your palm flat. She'll put her mouth on your hand, but she's not going to bite if your hand is flat and out of her way."

Reid grimaced but held the remainder of the carrot out to Buttercup. When her muzzle came in contact with his skin, he shivered and grabbed Walker's hand. "Oh my God, that feels so weird."

Buttercup nuzzled her head against Reid's chest as if asking for more carrots.

"See, she loves you now." Walker handed Reid another carrot. "Give her this one and then we'll walk her for a while."

A half hour later, all the carrots were gone and Buttercup was indeed loving Reid.

"She's not pushed me into the fence or stepped on my foot or kicked me even once," Reid marveled.

"Most horses are calm and sweet. Whatever horse horror movie you've got on replay isn't reality." Walker led Buttercup to the water trough. "You ready to put her away?"

Reid stood, hands on hips, and jutted his chin as he took a deep breath. "I want to ride."

"We will. Give yourself time."

"No, today. Unless you think I'm not ready." Reid walked slowly toward Walker and Buttercup. "She's the gentlest horse I've ever seen aside from Cinnamon. I want to start riding. Today."

"No reason not to, I just didn't want to push you too fast." Walker handed the lead to Reid. "Let her drink more if she wants. I'll get the tack, and we'll get started."

Two hours later, Reid was sore but exhilarated. "Was that okay? I mean, I know I still have to learn how to put on the saddle, but I think I did okay. What do you think?" His words were breathless as he led Buttercup back to the barn.

"You did great. I think your flexibility and rhythm from dance came in very handy. We'll work on it a bit each day until you're comfortable with a longer ride." Walker threw an arm around Reid's shoulders. "I'll show you how to brush her down and get her unsaddled."

Reid stopped at the entry to the barn and patted Buttercup before leaning his forehead against her neck. "Thanks, girl. You're the best." The horse nickered. "All the carrots in the world just for you. We're besties now."

"You may change your tune when you realize just how sore you're going to be tomorrow." Walker snickered.

Reid turned to face him. "First, thank you."

"For?"

"For teaching me, for being patient, for knowing she was perfect for me." Reid cupped Walker's cheek.

"And?"

"And, pretty sure I've done enough *riding* to know about the soreness. I'll be fine." Reid winked and brushed a kiss across Walker's lips.

Walker smirked. "Okay, cowboy. You let me know how that goes for you."

"ARE YOU OKAY?" Norma asked with genuine concern that evening. "Did you hurt yourself?"

"Just a little sore," Reid grimaced as he lowered himself into the seat at the kitchen table.

Walker snorted.

"What happened?" Norma frowned.

"Our boy decided he wanted to learn to ride." Walker reached over and patted Reid's hand and tried his best to hide a smile at Reid's snarl.

Norma beamed. "Really? That's amazing. So great!"

Then she winced. "Ah, so you're super saddle sore, huh?"

Reid's brows drew together, and he shifted in his seat. "Yeah, a lot more than I thought I would be. I mean, I'm used to...," he shot a glance at Walker, "used to *dancing* and thought I'd be better able to adjust to the saddle."

"Oh, sugar, the saddle is brutal." Norma clucked as she loaded the table with dinner. "My Benny had the hardest time. But let me tell you, the right hands with some liniment ointment is just what the doctor ordered."

Over the table, Reid met Walker's hot fiery gaze.

When dinner was complete, Norma bustled about cleaning up. "You boys go on out and finish up your evening chores. Walker, you remember where the liniment is?"

Walker swallowed thickly and nodded.

"A hot bath will ease the sore muscles, too." Norma nodded. "I'll be hitting the hay on my side of the house. Breakfast duties come early." She winked.

THE DOGS BOLTED into Reid's room when Walker nudged the door open.

"I'm dying," Reid groaned from his face-down position on the bed. "My ass and legs have never been this sore, and I didn't even get off from the experience."

Walker snorted back a laugh. "Aww, my poor cowboy," he crooned as he lay a hand on Reid's back. "How 'bout a hot bath with some soaking salts then I'll rub you down."

"And rub me off?" Reid suggested.

"You're incorrigible," Walker scolded. "I thought you were dying?"

"My dying wish is to get off with a hot cowboy."

"Well, if I see one around, I'll let you know," Walker teased.

"Stop, you know I mean you." Reid rolled to his side. "Whose idea was it for me to learn to ride a damn horse? I can't even try to seduce you into fucking me because my ass and legs already feel like I got fucked for a week by an angry gorilla going in dry."

Walker laughed out loud. "Calm down, cowboy. I'll go start the bath."

Five minutes later, Walker had the jacuzzi tub filling, bath salts sprinkled in, the lights dimmed, and a towel laid out.

"Want to get in with me?" Reid blushed as he hobbled into the bathroom.

Walker was quiet for a moment too long as if he was going to refuse, but then he bit his bottom lip and nodded before grabbing a towel for himself. He helped Reid into the warm water after the younger man removed his clothes.

"Oh my God, this feels amazing." Reid leaned back, but his hooded gaze was glued to Walker.

Walker stripped down quickly and climbed into the tub. Once he gently situated himself behind Reid, Walker pulled Reid's back to his chest.

"Mmm, feels even more amazing now," Reid moaned, his breath catching in his throat when Walker's hands grazed over his nipples and down to his abdomen.

"Let the heat of the water loosen your muscles," Walker murmured at Reid's ear before trailing light kisses down his jaw.

"Who knew water could act as a little prep and loosening?" Reid chuckled and let his head loll over so Walker could nibble and lick his neck.

"In case I haven't told you lately, I'm *really* glad you're here," Walker whispered. "You make me laugh and smile more than I can remember in my entire life."

"Even with Sam?" Reid covered Walker's hands with his own.

Walker was silent for a moment. "Yes, even with Sam."

"I'm sorry. You don't have to talk about him."

"No, it's okay." Walker tightened his arms around Reid and pulled him closer. "Sam was a great guy. I loved him without a doubt. But he wasn't silly and snarky like you. He was as smart as they came as far as ranchers, and he was an honest and hard worker. But he didn't light up a room like you do. He didn't make my heart sing like it sings when I'm with you."

"You don't have to compare us," Reid stated softly. "I know you loved him. You can love us the same or different." He tensed in Walker's arms. "I mean, not that I think you love me or anything."

"Shh, it's okay, I know what you meant."

Walker's words soothed. They were quiet for several heartbeats. Still in the silence, only their breaths and the occasional sound of water splashing filled the steamy air. They simply *were*. Reid and Walker. Together.

"I do, you know." Walker entwined his fingers with Reid's.

"Do what?" Reid sighed.

"Love you," Walker's words tickled at Reid's ear.

Reid turned his head and tipped his chin so he could see Walker's face. "You do?"

Walker nodded. "You had my interest the moment I saw you walking on that old dirt road. I think you had my heart the moment you dropped to your knees to pet the dogs."

"Me dropping to my knees gets a lot of people," Reid teased.

Walker smiled. "I fell for you bit by bit as I watched you with the dogs, with Norma, with Cinnamon. Seeing you settle in and be so warm and welcoming to the employees here and to the townspeople, it just wedged you deeper and deeper into my heart."

"So now I'm stuck there?"

"Yeah, I think you're a permanent fixture." Walker kissed Reid's head.

"Well, I think I make a great addition to your heart." Reid reached to pull Walker's face closer and kissed him. "And same."

"Same?"

"I love you too, cowboy," Reid whispered against Walker's lips. "Never in a million years did I think I'd find love and friendship way out on Pine Ridge Ranch, but I guess that's what happens when you think you know what your life has planned for you."

They sat in comfortable silence for a few minutes until Walker broke the moment. "As much as I hate to interrupt what we've got going here, the water is getting cold. Do you want more hot water, or are you ready to get out?"

"Depends."

"On?" Walker asked.

"If we get out, will you dance with me?" Reid sat up and turned around.

"Naked dancing?" Walker cocked his brow.

"Well, we *could* get dressed if you want." Reid shrugged. "But you promised me a rub down, so staying naked seems like a good plan."

"How 'bout I rub in the liniment first then we dance? That way it has time to soak in and hopefully help your pain while the muscles are still loose." Walker stood and exited the tub, wrapped his towel around his waist, and reached down to help Reid. "How are you feeling?"

Reid stood and accepted the towel Walker handed him. "Better. Still very sore, but the excruciating pain isn't as bad."

"Good, liniment and some anti-inflammatory pills before bed and you should be almost back to normal tomorrow." Walker winced. "Gotta tell you, though, the best way to get your body used to riding is to keep riding."

Reid whimpered. "Please don't mention climbing into a saddle right now. At least not a horse saddle." He wrapped his arms around Walker's neck and nuzzled. "But I could possibly be persuaded to climb onto a different animal and ride him hard."

"Duly noted, but I think you should hold off on any *vigorous* activities for tonight at least."

Reid pouted. "Fine. But we're still dancing."

"Lay down. I'll work the ointment in." Walker gestured toward the bed. "But take these ibuprofen first." He handed Reid the small pills and a disposable cup of water.

Reid threw back the pain relievers before he gingerly climbed onto the bed.

"Roll over first," Walker instructed. "I'll put down towels so the liniment doesn't get on the bed." He spread two large bath towels and then helped Reid roll to his stomach. Dipping his fingers into the tub of oint-ment, Walker started at Reid's calves and worked his way up. "Where's it hurt the worst?"

Reid moaned. "My upper legs, inner thighs, outer thighs, my ass, all of it."

Walker scooped more liniment and eased himself onto the bed to straddle Reid's legs.

"Oh my God," Reid's groaned words were muffled into the pillow, but the way he bucked and thrust his hips into the mattress spoke volumes.

"I wanted to straddle you like this the first time I rubbed you down," Walker's words were gruff as his hands massaged Reid's thighs.

"Dang it all to hell, why did I have to choose today to learn to ride?" Reid continued to pulse his hips into the towel. "I've never been so sore that I'd turn down a gorgeous cowboy at my ass."

"Well, you *are* that sore now, and I'd never even think of trying to take you this way when I know how badly you hurt." Walker's words were soft as he continued to work his hands into Reid's screaming muscles. "But I don't think a little fun would hurt too much." He took hold of Reid's plump ass and worked the fleshy globes in his hands like a baker kneading dough. "Roll over," Walker commanded.

Reid rolled over, his cock throbbing and hard against his stomach, his hooded gaze locking on Walker's already leaking dick as it bobbed proudly. "Sit on my chest. If you can't fuck my ass, I need you to at least fuck my mouth."

Walker straddled Reid's waist and then shimmied up Reid's chest. Before allowing Reid's hungry mouth to engulf his pulsing cock, Walker cupped Reid's cheek. "I've been tested, haven't been with anyone since Samuel."

Reid's eyes softened. "I know you'd never put me in danger. I'm all good, too," he murmured before licking his lips and taking Walker's length deep to the back of his throat.

Walker groaned and rocked his hips forward as Reid's hands came up to clutch at Walker's ass. At Reid's urging, Walker thrust his cock harder and faster into Reid's mouth. "Baby, I'm gonna come if I do this much longer," Walker muttered through gritted teeth.

Reid mumbled around a mouth full of cock before releasing Walker long enough to speak. "Do it. Come for me. I want to taste you, swallow you." Reid licked Walker and sucked on his head before opening for Walker to continue fucking his mouth. Reid moved his hands from Walker's muscular ass to slightly lower to fondle Walker's drawn-up balls.

"Ah, God, so good. Your mouth is so damn good," Walker bit out as he thrust his cock over and over between Reid's plump pink lips. "You're gonna swallow me down, and then I'll make you come like never before. I'll suck your cock and lick your ass so good, baby."

Walker continued to pump, and Reid whimpered at Walker's dirty words until Walker gave one last thrust and froze as he poured himself down Reid's greedy throat.

Reid licked Walker cleaned, and then they shared the bounty in a messy, salty, sticky kiss.

Walker shifted from sitting on Reid's chest to lay on top of the smaller man, allowing the kiss to continue, deepening and growing hotter as Reid's cock pulsed between them. Walker moved to sit up and straddle Reid's knees before grasping Reid's upper thighs and digging in with gentle, deep motions to loosen the aching muscles.

"Suck me, please," Reid begged.

Walker bent slowly and took Reid's cock in his mouth, swirling his tongue around the head before taking it to the back of his throat. Popping off of Reid's throbbing dick, Walker moved from his position on Reid's legs. "Do you think you can spread your legs and lift them? Or do you want to roll over?"

Reid wordlessly rolled over and lifted his ass in the air, a beautiful offering just for Walker.

"So fucking gorgeous," Walker whispered before spreading Reid's cheeks slightly and licking into his hole.

Reid called out, his garbled words ending in whimpers and sobs as Walker continued to probe his hot tongue in and around Reid's pucker. When Walker reached to pump Reid's dick, Reid rolled away. "Wait, stop."

Walker stopped immediately. "What, baby? Did I do something wrong? Are you hurting?"

Reid panted and held a hand to his cock. "No, but I was about to come, and I want to dance first." He blushed and glanced shyly at Walker. "Because after I come, I'm going to get sleepy, and I want to curl up in your arms all night. But not before we dance."

Walker leaned in to kiss him. "Let's dance then," he growled.

Reid quickly found a playlist on his phone as Walker dimmed the lights.

"Never danced naked before," Walker murmured as he took Reid into his arms.

Reid wrapped his arms around Walker's neck, kissing him as they pressed their bodies together and swayed to the soft music. Reid nuzzled against Walker's chest, breathing deeply. His lips grazed Walker's skin. "I love you," he whispered before his body shuddered as he sobbed.

"Hey," Walker crooned lifting Reid's head with a finger under his chin. "Baby, what's wrong?"

Reid shook his head and sniffled. "Nothing, not a damn thing. I've never felt so loved, welcomed, or completely at home. I can't believe I ever considered leaving this place, leaving you." He rested his elbows on Walker's shoulders, his hands behind Walker's head, and leaned his forehead against Walker's chin. "If Grandpa Jack hadn't orchestrated all of this, I would have missed out on true love and happiness. I'm just overwhelmed at how different things could have turned out."

"Shhh," Walker kissed the top of Reid's head and hugged him closer. "Jack, Norma, fate, God, whoever you want to name, they all knew what they were doing." Walker took Reid's head in his palms. "I love you as much as I love this ranch life. I'd like to think we would have found each other no matter what, but I'm so very grateful for whatever brought you into my life. I was only going through the motions before you, you gave me reason to love and live and be happy."

Reid choked back a sob. "I love you. I was drifting through life, not sad, not overly happy. I was helping, but I didn't feel needed. I didn't feel a reason to exist. Until I found you and this place." He lifted his face, tears streaming down his cheeks.

Walker wiped Reid's tears with his thumbs before capturing Reid's mouth in a desperate kiss and maneuvering their position to the side of the bed. "Soon, I'm going to lay you down in bed and lick every damn part of you, eat that ass like it's the last meal I'll ever have, and make love to you, fuck you, make you mine in every damn sense of the word."

Reid's body shivered in Walker's arms as his lover's words sunk in. "Yes, please...," Reid groaned.

Walker lay Reid down on the bed and growled in his ear, "Until then, we're going to rub against each other like two horny teens until you come all over me."

"God, yes," Reid moaned and rocked his hips into Walker's.

"I love you, love holding you, love tasting you, love coming for you," Walker whispered as he thrust his cock against Reid's again and again. "Want to make you come, want to finger your ass, stretch you, fill your body with my cock." Walker shuddered, tripping over his words, "Fuck I'm gonna come."

"Again?" Reid panted, his nails digging into Walker's ass as he pulled him tighter and pumped their cocks together.

"That's what you do to me, baby," Walker bit out. "Come for me, paint me. I want your come mixed with mine, coating our bodies."

Reid thrust one more time, his body tensing as his release spread between them, his head thrown back, his whimpers filling the air.

Walker bit Reid's exposed neck and groaned as his own release melded with Reid's. Walker swirled his finger in the mixture before smearing a drop on Reid's full bottom lip and swooping in to kiss it from Reid's mouth, both men moaning at their mixed essence.

Several moments later when their breathing had returned to somewhat normal, Reid shifted. "Grab a washcloth, please."

Walker wet two cloths with warm water and cleaned them up.

Reid threw the bath towels to the ground and pulled back the covers. "Will you sleep in here tonight?" Reid held out a hand.

Walker took Reid's hand and crawled into bed. "I'll sleep wherever you are every night for the rest of my life if you'll have me."

Reid smiled through tears and allowed himself to be wrapped in Walker's arms only moments before sleep overtook him.

## 13

"Boss, we got a problem." Wes stuck his head in the office the next morning as Reid and Walker were going over paperwork.

"What's up?" Walker asked.

"Found two heifers dead out in the pasture." Wes entered the room and removed his hat, a frown worrying his face.

"Well, shit. Two? That's not normal." Walker ran a hand over his face. "Lightning?"

"No, that's the most troubling part," Wes answered. "Definitely not an accident; their throats were slit."

"The hell?" Walker shot out of his chair. "Animal attack?"

"No way." Wes shook his head. "These cuts were way too neat and clean."

"Then what?"

"Looks like a knife or something similar." Wes winced. "Gruesome sight. Zeke and I found them when we noticed we didn't have the whole herd."

"Who the hell would cut the neck of a couple cows? That's fuckin' insane," Walker grumbled and shoved a hand through his hair.

Reid lay a hand on Walker's shoulder. "I think we may have a pretty good guess of where to start."

Walker turned with wide eyes. "Shit, you don't think he had something to do with it?"

Reid shrugged. "Probably not first-hand, but I'd bet he's involved somewhere down the chain of command."

Walker was silent for a moment before taking a deep breath and crossing his arms across his chest. "Well, with the geothermal company making noise and now this, I guess it would make sense."

"What do we do?" Reid asked.

"Okay Wes, first, let's call the cops. I want a detailed report filed. Then take the men out and get the animals cleaned up. Step up the perimeter runs and be sure everyone is keeping an eye out for anything or anyone out of the ordinary." Walker reached for his hat. "We need to make sure Norma and the rest of the crew knows to use extra precaution. Wes you'll be in charge until we get back."

"Where are we going?" Reid asked.

"Looks like we'll be moving up our meeting with the geothermal company." Walker followed Wes and Reid out of the office. "I'll have the truck gassed up and fill in Norma. You pack a bag. Once I throw some things together, I'll let my grandmother know the new plan and we'll head out."

"Think we should call the company and let them know we're coming?" Reid slowed to fall in step beside Walker.

"Nah, no reason to give them time to prepare." Walker paused to shake Wes's hand and slap him on the shoulder before continuing to the house with Reid. "Throw them off guard, and see if we can catch them in some lies or if they're up to no good. Plus, we don't want to tip your dad off. If he's part of this, we need to do what we can to keep the upper hand."

Within an hour, the ranch was informed and stepped up security measures were set into motion. Walker or Reid threw their bags in the truck and hit the road.

"Does any of this seem...I don't know, just fucking surreal?" Reid asked as they traveled down the long expanse of highway.

"Surreal? Yeah, I can see that." Walker nodded.

"It's just, I had no desire to own a ranch, visit a ranch, hell, even step *foot* on a ranch." Reid shifted in his seat and faced Walker. "It's not like I had my whole future mapped out. I wanted to dance, help people, and get the hell away from my father. Not necessarily in that order. But now I'm the owner of a ranch, in love with the foreman, learning to ride fucking horses, and preparing for a battle with an unknown threat who is very likely my own father." Reid shook his head. "So damn surreal. My life has taken paths I didn't even know existed."

"Guess we can't plan our lives down to the minute details." Walker shrugged. "Never thought I'd be praying some city boy with a flair for fashion would want to own the ranch. Never planned to fall in love again; didn't think I needed or wanted love again. Definitely never planned to be facing off with a disgruntled man throwing a dangerous hissy fit and messing with the lives of my animals and employees." Walker patted the seat next to him, and Reid scooted over. "Jack *never* wanted the ranch to be sold. Not to the bank, a geothermal company, not to anyone. I plan to stick to what Jack would have wanted for Pine Ridge."

"I mean, isn't it just as easy as saying 'No' to the geothermal people?" Reid lay his head on Walker's shoulder.

"Yes and no." Walker shifted to put his right arm around Reid and his left hand on the wheel. "We can tell them no. They can continue pursuing us if they choose. Some companies are ruthless. We aren't on that large of a geothermal pocket, not sure why they'd be *that* set on getting our land. But if Daddy Jack has his hand in the pot, he may be stirring up their interest and providing incentive to land the deal. The company and Jack could start digging up history on the land and ranch and find even the smallest iota of a detail that could put us in a bad spot."

"The ranch has been run spotlessly for decades ever since Grandpa Jack took over, you said so yourself." Reid reached to adjust the air conditioning vent. "PS... I'm glad we brought the newer truck. A road trip in Bert would have been a hot mess."

Walker chuckled. "Agreed. That's why Bert is a ranch truck only. And you're right, the ranch has been in tiptop condition since Jack took over, but before that it may have had some issues. Maybe some bad business deals, late loan payments, and bad experiences for employees. The company could dig any and all of that up and use it to drag the Pine Ridge name through the mud and get us stuck in legal proceedings for years."

"That was decades ago and the ranch runs on the up and up now. Who would care?"

"Most people wouldn't give two shits. But if your dad and the company are determined enough, they could make it into a bigger issue than what it really is." Walker drew in a deep breath. "I'd really like to think the company isn't in a desperate position and will eventually tell your dad to take a hike."

"Yeah, let's hope." Reid sighed. "But my dad doesn't

give up super easily. His tenacity and aggressiveness is mostly why he's such a mogul in the in the business world. He attacks hard, chews them up, and then spits them out."

"And doesn't give a damn who he hurts in the process," Walker grumbled.

"Not for a single nanosecond," Reid replied. "And he's likely embarrassed by the fact his father bucked such a long-standing tradition and slighted him by handing the ranch to me. So he's got to save face along with landing a big deal."

"Great. Can't wait for the meeting."

Reid was silent for about a mile. "Maybe I should just sell to him?" he whispered.

"What?" Walker boomed. "No way. Why would you even think that?"

"Just a passing thought, never mind." Reid kissed Walker on the cheek.

"Well, be sure any thoughts like that keep right on passin' on," Walker stated gruffly.

"So, what's our plan with this whole trip?" Reid changed the subject, he didn't want to dwell on his father and the option to sell.

"We'll stay at a hotel tonight, and try to prep ourselves for the meeting. Visit with my grandma after we meet with the company. Do one more night in the hotel then head home." Walker kissed the top of Reid's head. "Sound okay to you?"

"Sounds delightful. Minus the part about meeting with the company."

"You'll be able to wear one of the fancier outfits you bought," Walker offered. "I hope you packed something dressy."

"Oh..." Reid clasped his hands together. "That's definitely a positive. And of course I packed something fancy. I have been wanting to wear something a little more fashionable than jeans and boots."

"You're the most fashionable that ranch has ever seen," Walker assured.

"Why, thank you very much," Reid gushed. "It's nice to have my sense of fashion appreciated."

"I definitely appreciate it, but I'd love looking at you in absolutely anything." Walker paused and cocked his head. "Better yet, in nothing at all," he teased. "And I'm sure the horses look forward to your outfit choices on a daily basis. The rest of the ranch, I'm not so sure about."

Reid laughed. "Wrong. Norma likes to see my clothes. So do some of the wives. Pretty sure Zeke likes them too but he'd never admit it."

"At least not yet." Walker sighed. "I worry about that kid. He's got so much bottled up, he's going to explode."

"Agreed. He seems like an intelligent and good-hearted kid, but he's dealing with a lot right now. I think he's questioning his sexuality, he feels stuck between two races, he's not the same age as most the people on the ranch." Reid sat up and stretched a bit. "I think he'll feel so much more at home in his own skin if and when he's able to accept the real him. But until then, it's a hard road. He's young, it's normal to question. But I feel like he's so far in the closet that he may never find his way out. And forcing a person to admit something they aren't ready to admit or accept is never a good idea."

"Yeah, I can't decide if I think he'll eventually come around or if he'll just keep hiding it from himself and the world." Walker switched hands on the steering wheel and leaned his left arm on the door. "Having you around is probably the best thing that could have happened to him. Maybe seeing you happy and successful and in a relationship will make it easier for him."

"You think he'll stay on the ranch or bolt as soon as he's able?" Reid mused.

"I think he'd bolt in a heartbeat except he's so attached to Shay, Elise, and the upcoming baby that he probably feels somewhat tied to the ranch. Even if he ever left, I think his family would pull him back." Walker pointed toward a road sign. "Says we've got about five miles to our exit. We'll find a hotel, get settled, find something to eat, and then explore the town."

"Can we go dancing?"

Walker's eyeroll could practically be heard in the truck cab. "We'll see if we can find a gay bar with dancing."

"Sweetie, the words *gay bar* pretty much guarantee dancing." Reid shoulder bumped Walker. "And it doesn't *have* to be a gay bar. Just find me some drinks and dancing, and I'll be a happy homo."

"I'd feel safer with a gay bar. Not all places are as accepting as Pine Ridge."

"Don't I know it," Reid whispered. "We can search once we get Wi-Fi. Dear God, please tell me the hotel will have Wi-Fi."

Walker laughed. "It should. You'll be able to use your actual phone rather than one of the ranch phones."

Reid pulled his phone from his pocket. "Yes, yes, my sweet baby. I know, Daddy's missed you too. Soon, baby girl, we'll be reconnected soon."

Walker shook his head.

## 14

"I t's not up to LA standards, but I think it's a pretty nice room." Walker tossed his duffel bag on the chair and opened the curtain.

"Eh, LA standards are overrated." Reid threw his overnight bag next to Walker's and walked up behind his cowboy. Wrapping his arms around Walker's waist, Reid snuggled into his back. "Besides, in a LA hotel I would be there alone or with some pointless, shallow hookup. Here I'm with you and that makes it a thousand times better."

"Aww, such a sweet talker." Walker turned in Reid's arms and held him close. "We've got free Wi-Fi, a king-sized bed, and a very large shower, plus a great view of the city. I'm not sure what else two visiting gay men could ask for." Walker kissed Reid softly at first and then applied more pressure and probed Reid's mouth with his tongue.

Reid reached up and tangled his arms around Walker's neck. "Maybe some showtunes? A Broadway musical? Mimosas by the pool and a champagne brunch?"

"You're very good." Walker teased and nibbled at Reid's lips. "You just fit four stereotypes into one sentence."

Reid chuckled. "I'm damn good. And it's about time you found out just how damn good I am." He rocked his hips into Walker's and kissed him deeply.

Walker maneuvered them closer to the bed and gave Reid a little shove. "Agreed. Show me whatcha got."

"Strip," Reid commanded before pulling off his own clothes without ever taking his eyes from Walker. Then he sat on the edge of the bed and lay back.

When Walker was naked, he climbed onto the bed, straddling Reid's hips.

Reid gripped Walker's ass and pulled him forward. Not taking his gaze from Walker's, Reid licked his lips before slowly taking Walker's cock into his mouth. Walker leaned his arms on the headboard and fucked long and slow into Reid's greedy mouth several times before pulling out and rolling from his position to lay on the bed.

"Come here, baby. Sit that pretty ass right here," Walker commanded as he patted his chest.

Reid climbed on Walker's chest, his ass facing Walker's head, and leaned forward to suck Walker's dick while fondling his balls.

The first lick of Walker's tongue against Reid's ass brought a low groan from both men.

Walker tongued Reid's hole and stroked Reid's cock.

Reid took each thrust of Walker's hard length deep to the back of his throat.

With a slight shift, the men turned to their sides and continued to feast upon each other.

Walker slicked his finger alongside Reid's cock before moving to tease Reid's ass.

Both men rocked their hips forward, thrusting hard and fast.

As Walker's finger breached Reid's hole, the younger man tensed and spilled his release a moment before Walker roared and exploded with his own.

THE MEN DOZED for an hour or so before rousing themselves to wash and get ready to go out.

"Save water and shower with me?" Reid waggled his brows as he turned on the nozzle.

"Conservation is important," Walker teased and followed Reid into the large walk-in shower.

"Oh my God, I love the double showerheads. It's like being under a warm waterfall." Reid let one of the showers of water soak his face and head.

Walker did the same at the other spray before turning to wrap his arms around Reid's waist. "Mmmm, I love the double shower head, too. I'm thinking our bathrooms at the ranch need them installed." He kissed Reid's neck and licked at the water rivulets before nibbling at Reid's ear. "I like that I can kiss you, lick you, suck you, and never be out of the water. We can stand like this and my back isn't freezing because you're hogging the water."

"You forgot one thing you can do." Reid reached up, wrapping his arms over his head to grasp Walker's head, and rubbed his ass against Walker's steely length. He gasped when Walker wrapped one hand around Reid's cock and used the other hand to tease his nipples.

"What did I forget?" Walker's words rumbled at Reid's ear.

"Fuck me...you can shove me against the wall and fuck me until my knees give out and the water runs cold." Reid panted as he fisted a hand in Walker's hair and pumped his cock in Walker's hand.

"Silly me, how could I forget that part?" Walker whispered. "But I have no plans to fuck you in the shower."

Reid whimpered and thrust his hips in frustration.

"Shhh, it's okay, baby. I want that beautiful ass just as badly as you want me there. But I'll take you for the first time in a bed, like a gentleman." Walker moved his hand from Reid's nipples and cupped his balls while continuing to stroke his cock.

"I don't need a gentleman. Feel free to ravage me," Reid whined.

"Oh, I will." Walker kept up a slow pumping with his fist. "But the first time I own your ass will be in a bed."

"So old fashioned," Reid sassed. "You going to demand our *love making* be slow and gentle too?"

"Every time I touch you, whether soft and slow or hard and fast, in bed or in a shower, on the bed of a truck or the ground under the stars, rest assured that I'll be making love to you." Walker squeezed Reid's cock gently and ran a wet finger between Reid's ass cheeks. "Come for me, baby. I can tell you're close. Let it go."

Reid reached out to steady himself with one arm and held tight to Walker's arm across his chest with the other before rocking his hips once, twice, three times and coming in his lover's hand with a soft moan.

"Something tells me we're using up more water showering together than if we had showered separately," Walker teased.

"Then I better get you off quickly before we lose hot water." Reid turned and began to drop to his knees, but Walker stopped him. "What's wrong?"

"Nothing. But I'm good." Walker pulled him in for a kiss. "Good things come to those who wait."

Reid pouted.

"I'll be all the more ready to get you back here tonight and pound your ass until you're walking funny," Walker cooed.

Reid brightened. "True that. Okay, let's finish this up. Dinner, drinks, and dancing await us and those aren't even the best of the four D's."

"Four D's?"

"Dinner, drinks, dancing, and *dick*. That last one is my favorite. I've always been fond of all four, but until you, dancing and dick were in a pretty tight race, but now that I have your dick in my life, it's definitely coming out on top," Reid explained.

"Mmm, *coming* out on top, sounds like a plan to me." Walker kissed Reid once more and slapped his ass. "Come on, cowboy, let's head 'em up and move 'em out."

Reid looked to the ceiling. "I tried to *head him*, but noooo."

Walker rolled his eyes and reached for the shampoo.

In a small booth at the edge of the bar's dance floor, Reid scooted as close to Walker as possible. "Oh my God, I still can't stop laughing about our server at dinner."

"She was something else, huh?" Walker chuckled.

"It was bad enough when she was all giggly and making googly eyes at you," Reid said. "But when she asked if we wanted to wait for our girlfriends before we ordered, I thought I would fall out of my seat." Reid laughed. "The look on her face when you grabbed my hand and told her we were ready to order was absolutely priceless."

"Welcome to the norm for this area." Walker shrugged. "Members of the LGBT+ community aren't often welcomed or accepted. I'd be willing to bet we were the first 'real-life' gay couple that girl had ever seen. She'll probably tell the story to all her friends."

"At least she stopped flirting once she realized we were together," Reid mused. "Would have been totally weird if she had kept on hitting on you while you held my hand."

Walker glanced around the bar. "So, it's probably not the gay bar you were hoping for, but at least it's reputed to be gay friendly."

"There's alcohol, music, and a dance floor." Reid wiggled in his seat. "It will do just fine."

Just then a server placed two frosty mugs of beer on their table with a smile and a wink. "Compliments of myself and the bartender," he quipped. "You boys let me know if you're looking for a little fun later. Brandon and I get off around one o'clock, and we'd be more than happy to show y'all around town." He stuck out his hand. "My name is Gage, by the way."

Walker and Reid shook the younger man's hand.

"Thanks for the beers and the offer," Reid started.

"But we need to be in fairly early tonight," Walker continued. "We've got some business to attend to early in the morning."

Gage pursed his lips. "Shame," he drawled. "Let me know if you change your minds."

"Will do," Walker agreed.

Reid took several swallows of his beer before he snorted and hid his face in his hands. "I swear, this night keeps getting funnier."

"I don't think I've ever been hit on this much," Walker agreed. "Your presence must be the difference."

Reid sobered a moment. "Did you want to take Brandon and Gage up on their offer?" He glanced at the two men now chatting and flirting with each other behind the bar. "Not really my thing, but I won't stop you."

Walker frowned. "Are you kidding me?" He put an arm around Reid's shoulders. "First, I'm pretty sure they were mostly interested in getting *you* between them. Second, you're plenty for me to handle all by yourself." Walker kissed Reid's temple. "Group sex may have seemed like the ultimate fantasy when I was younger, but it doesn't float my boat these days."

"Good to know," Reid whispered and brushed his lips over Walker's, "because I have no desire to share you with anyone. Especially two guys as hot as Brandon and Gage over there." Reid inclined his head toward the bar and waggled his fingers toward the two men.

"You're bad," Walker growled into Reid's mouth.

"What? I'm just letting them know we're good."
Reid broke the kiss. "Let's finish this beer, which tastes
like piss by the way, and then get our dance on."

"How would you know what piss tastes like?"
Walker cocked a brow. "You know what, never mind,
don't answer that."

"What?" Reid frowned. "Wait, *what?* No,
eeewwww. That's not a kink I fancy." Reid shuddered.

Walker laughed. "I wouldn't judge you, but we're on
the same page with that one." He drained his beer.
"Come on, cowboy, let's get our dance on."

"Um, so the music here is quite...," Reid hung on
Walker's back as they walked to join the dancers on the
floor, "...what's the word I'm looking for?"

Walker turned around to find Reid's face puckered
up like he'd sucked a lemon wedge. "Quite country?"
Walker suggested.

Reid winced and nodded. "I didn't notice at first,
but these definitely aren't my usual dance tunes." His
eyes widened as the song changed and the dancers scurried to form four lines. "Oh. My. God. Are they line
dancing?"

Walker threw back his head and laughed. "Welcome to the country my little city boy." He grabbed
Reid's hand and pulled him onto the floor. "Now this is
the type of dancing I can handle. Watch them and you'll
pick it up quickly."

Reid took his place next to Walker and stumbled through a few steps before catching onto the rhythm and pattern of the dance. Reid laughed and shouted, "Yee-haw! We should have worn our hats."

Four songs later, Walker drug Reid from the floor. "I'm dying. I need a drink."

"Water then beer and one more dance," Reid begged.

"Agreed." Walker waved at the girl behind the bar and ordered two waters and two beers. "One more dance, but then we leave. I've got a treat for you back at the hotel."

"Mmm, I like treats." Reid drained his water. "Wait, is treat a euphemism for dick? Because that's the treat I want."

"No," Walker nearly choked on his water, "the treat isn't dick. You can have dick *and* the treat."

Reid waggled his brows as he took several swallows from his beer bottle. "Dick and treats? This night just keeps getting better and better." He tipped up the bottom of Walker's bottle. "Drink up, baby."

*My Best Friend* by Tim McGraw began to play. Walker gave Reid a questioning look. "Slow song or wait for another line dance?"

Reid winked and took Walker's hand as they walked to the dance floor.

They took their place among the other couples swaying slowly to the country ballad.

"This song is sort of perfect, ya know?" Reid spoke at Walker's ear.

"Yeah?" Walker tightened his arms around Reid's waist.

"Listen to the words," Reid instructed. "More than a lover, you're my best friend. That's us. I mean, at least for me."

Walker smiled and kissed Reid's temple. "For me, too."

When the song ended, Walker took Reid's hand and led him out the door.

"What's my treat?" Reid asked.

"Patience, cowboy, you'll get it soon enough." Walker smacked Reid's ass.

"COME HERE, baby, I've got some sugar for you." Walker's gruff words sounded in the softly lit room as Reid emerged from the bathroom.

Reid smiled coyly as he dropped his towel and sauntered to the bed. "Mmm, give me some sugar." He climbed onto the bed.

Walker wrestled Reid onto his back. "I'm in charge. You behave and you'll get your treat."

Reid whimpered.

When Walker slid a silk blindfold over Reid's eyes,

Reid whispered, "Holy shit, what kind of kinky fuckery is this?"

Reid's excitement grew when Walker forced his arms over his head and tied his wrists together.

"Don't move your arms," Walker commanded. "You don't get to touch right now."

Walker's lips came down on Reid's mouth, crushing and wet.

Reid returned the kiss hungrily until Walker pulled away and left the bed.

"Oh God, Walker, don't leave me like this," Reid whined.

"Shhh," Walker shushed as he returned to Reid's side of the bed.

A rough sensation touched Reid's lips, and he startled before automatically sticking out his tongue to taste. Walker continued to rub something along Reid's lips as Reid continued to lick and moan and his body writhed on the mattress.

"You like that sugar, baby?" Walker moved the rough material over Reid's nipples.

"Is that real sugar?" Reid asked. "Oh my God," Reid panted as sugar granules berated his flesh.

"Sugar cube like we fed Buttercup. Some sugar for my sugar," Walker whispered before taking Reid's mouth in his and cleaning the sugar from Reid's lips.

Their tongues met in a sweet and sticky dance.

Walker broke the kiss and trailed his lips down to lick the sugar from Reid's nipples.

Reid bucked his hips and whimpered. "Please," he begged.

"Please what?" Walker continued to tongue at Reid's pink pebbled nipples.

"Fuck me," Reid commanded. "Please, fuck me now, or I'm going to come."

Walker chuckled. "Oh, you're going to come. That's for sure. But you won't come until I'm deep inside that gorgeous ass."

"Now, please now," Reid continued to beg.

Walker moved from the bed, and Reid heard the thump of what he assumed was a bottle of lube landing on the side table.

"Take off the blindfold, please?" Reid asked. "I want to see you the first time you fuck me."

"Well, that's too bad," Walker answered gruffly. "Because I'm not fucking you." He reached to remove the blindfold and wrist tie and kissed Reid deeply. Walker rested his forehead on Reid's. "Remember, whether hard and fast or long and slow, any time I *fuck* you, I'll be making *love* to you. Because I love you," he declared and attacked Reid's mouth again.

Reid spread his legs, and Walker nestled their hips together.

"I love you so much," Reid murmured against Walker's lips.

Walker lifted Reid's legs and spread his knees. "God, baby, look at your ass. So pretty, so ready for me." Walker licked his finger and trailed it along Reid's hole.

Reid took hold of his own legs. "Please, please," he chanted.

Walker grabbed lube from the bedside tabletop and slicked himself and Reid before pressing the head of his cock at Reid's pucker. He held his breath as he pushed forward slowly, waiting for Reid's body to open for him.

"Oh God, yes, so good," Reid moaned and threw his head back.

"Look at you opening for me. Taking me so deep," Walker gritted the words through his teeth as he watched his cock sink farther into Reid's ass. When he was fully engulfed by Reid's body, Walker leaned forward and wrapped Reid in his arms while pumping his dick long and slow.

"Come in me. I want to feel your cock throbbing," Reid begged.

"Stroke yourself and come with me," Walker commanded as he pushed up on his arms and continued thrusting.

Reid took his cock in his hand and began to pump to Walker's rhythm.

"Yes, baby, just like that. Jack that gorgeous cock." Walker bit out his words and increased his speed. "I'm going to come, watching you like this," he warned.

"Do it," Reid urged. "Come in me."

With a final thrust, Walker unloaded with a long groan, his cock spurting and throbbing as Reid's ass milked the final drops from him. Walker stilled and breathed heavily as he watched Reid stroke himself to completion. When Reid painted his release over his torso, Walker ran a finger through it and sucked his finger into his mouth before leaning in and kissing Reid.

A few seconds later, he collapsed onto Reid with a moan.

Reid echoed the sound. "That was fucking amazing. Like, I'm not even exaggerating, I've never had better sex."

Walker lifted his head and frowned. "Why do I hear a but in there?"

"My legs are killing me. Get off me you big oaf." Reid gave Walker a shove as they both laughed.

"God, don't do that. You had me worried something was wrong," Walker grumbled as he pulled from Reid's body.

"There was, my legs were going to start spasming or something," Reid teased as he rolled from the bed and limped to the bathroom. "Oh my God, I may never walk the same again."

Walker laughed and threw a pillow at him. "Clean yourself and bring me a towel please."

"Just because you owned my ass just now doesn't mean you can order me around," Reid sassed from the bathroom.

"I said please," Walker hollered back, a smile in his words.

A wet cloth smacked him in the face.

"Hey!" Walker shouted. "Totally not necessary!" But he laughed and wiped himself down.

Reid returned to the bed a few minutes later. "Sleep. Must sleep."

The men curled together under the blanket and where asleep within minutes.

"ARE YOU SUPER SORE?" Walker whispered at Reid's ear early the next morning, his big spoon protectively curled around Reid's small spoon.

Reid grumbled, and shimmied his ass against Walker's cock. "A little, but it's a good hurt. Just be gentle."

Walker slicked Reid's entrance with a spit-wet finger before lifting Reid's leg to drape over his own hip. Walker pressed, gentle and slow, until Reid's body relaxed and allowed him in.

In their sleepy states, the men slowly thrust and rocked, quietly groaned and whispered their love for each other, gently stroked and kissed until their bodies found long, slow, gentle releases.

"I will never get tired of having you in my ass or of you holding me in your arms," Reid stated sleepily.

"Good to know," Walker replied, "because I'll never get tired of being in your ass or having you in my arms."

After they found release once more, they slept, wrapped in a cocoon of arms and legs, sticky and sated until an alarm sounded to rouse them for their meeting.

A WOMAN GLANCED up from computer to greet them as they entered the office. "Welcome to Northern Plains Geothermal."

"Good morning, Charlene," Walker greeted the woman at the front desk cheerfully after glancing at her nametag. "Walker Corrigan and Reid Alexander here to see Mr. Stewart," Walker stated with a friendly yet firm tone.

"Is Mr. Stewart expecting you?" Charlene inquired.

"No, ma'am, he's not. We have a meeting scheduled in a couple weeks, but some recent developments require that be moved up." Walker crossed his arms. "Please let Mr. Stewart know we're here."

"This is highly unusual and outside of protocol," Charlene huffed.

"I can assure you Mr. Stewart will be interested in seeing us."

Charlene pursed her lips before standing from her chair and scuttling toward the double doors labeled *Northern Plains Geothermal, Mr. David Stewart.*

Reid snorted, and Walker grabbed his elbow to steer him to the waiting room chairs.

"She's got a corncob stuck where the sun don't shine," Reid muttered in a mock drawl.

Walker nudged him. "Shhhh," he whispered.

"You think he'll let us in or refuse to see us?" Reid crossed a fashionably trousered leg over his knee and primped the sleeves of his dress shirt.

"I think he will probably contact your father and then allow us in to see what we want." Walker shrugged. "His curiosity will be too much to send us away."

"Unless my dad happens to be in South Dakota right now, we at least won't have to endure that unpleasantness," Reid stated.

They sat for fifteen minutes, soft music playing over the speakers, the scent of coffee filling the air, and a small television playing a video boasting the benefits of geothermal heat.

The doors swung open, and Charlene emerged, looking as if she had noticed the scent of dog droppings. "Mr. Stewart will see you now." She stood with the door open for the men and stared straight ahead as they walked by.

"Mr. Corrigan, pleasure to see you again," Mr. Stewart gushed as he gripped Walker's hand. "Mr. Alexander, so pleased to make your acquaintance. Your father has told me many things about his only son." Mr. Stewart shook Reid's hand.

"I can only imagine the stories you've heard," Reid replied with a sardonic smile.

"Have a seat, gentlemen." Mr. Stewart gestured. "Forgive me for appearing unprepared. I was of course pleased to move our meeting earlier, but the lack of communication put me in a bit of a bind. Please allow me a moment to pull up the Pine Ridge files."

"We appreciate you moving the meeting," Walker took a seat at the head of the conference table. "This meeting shouldn't take long."

Reid sat at Walker's right. "Pardon me for being so blunt, but what relationship does Northern Plains Geothermal have with my father, sir?"

Mr. Stewart's face blanched as he fiddled with the computer files.

Walker cast a sly smile Reid's way.

"Ah, yes, here it is." Mr. Stewart sputtered and avoided the question. "Pine Ridge Ranch. Such a prime piece of land with tremendous potential in the world of geothermal heat."

"What exactly is your interest in our land?" Reid asked. "From what Mr. Corrigan has shown me and shared with me, Pine Ridge *does* sit on a geothermal pocket, but it's not large compared to the pockets Northern Plains Geothermal usually mines."

Mr. Stewart nodded. "I agree that the pocket under Pine Ridge isn't the biggest we've ever gone after. However, your ranch would provide us with prime land after the mining, and we would use that for expanding our business."

"So, you want to buy Pine Ridge, put ranch employees out of jobs, and destroy the land for a pocket of heat, and then reuse our land to build your business?" Walker frowned and scratched at the back of his head. "Just doesn't seem to benefit anyone but Northern Plains Geothermal if you want to know the truth."

"Mr. Corrigan, the amount Northern Plains Geothermal is willing to pay for Pine Ridge is sizable. Money wouldn't be an issue for you if you sell." Mr. Stewart leaned back in his chair, a smarmy smile on his face.

"We," Reid corrected. "If *we* sell, which we have no plans to do, *we* would perhaps get a sizable chunk of money. But what about our ranch employees? Their families? Not to mention an area of land that has been in my family for generations being mined and then turned into plot and parcel for building a mining business. Money isn't our biggest worry." Reid shook his head. "And what does Jack Alexander have to do with your company?" Reid persisted.

"Mr. Alexander is a dedicated, generous donor and has consistently supported Northern Plains Geothermal." Mr. Stewart smiled broadly like the Cheshire cat. "We are blessed to have such a brilliant businessman and benefactor in our corner."

"Blessed enough to stoop to unprofessional means to gain ownership of the Pine Ridge?" Reid countered.

Mr. Stewart's mousy face turned a plum purple as he stammered, "Mr. Alexander, I'm sure I have not the slightest idea what you're insinuating."

"Let me rephrase," Reid interrupted. "My father has been pissed I inherited my grandfather's ranch since the day of the will reading. Now you're back to hounding Mr. Corrigan for the ranch and some animals have been slaughtered. Seems like too much of a coincidence that my father is one of your supportive donors and now these issues are occurring. May I ask when you brought Mr. Alexander on as a benefactor?"

"We formed a partnership with Mr. Alexander not long ago, but the exact details are none of your business, and I'm highly offended that you would think Northern Plains Geothermal would do anything unbecoming." Mr. Stewart seemed to find a bit of a backbone as he leaned his elbows on the desk and stared at Reid and Walker.

"What I know is that the late Jackson Alexander wanted nothing to do with your company and told you so on many occasions." Walker crossed his arms. "I also know I have two animals with their throats slit. That, and your renewed interest in the ranch, coincide with the arrival of Mr. Alexander's son arriving and taking his place as legal owner of the Pine Ridge." Walker cocked his head. "Surely you can see why Reid and I are concerned."

Mr. Stewart steepled his fingers at his chin and narrowed his eyes. "What I know, gentlemen, is that the Pine Ridge ranch sits over a pocket of geothermal heat energy that Northern Plains Geothermal would very much like to acquire. Mr. Jackson has come on to our business team to assist in tightening up our acquisitions, our holdings, our financials, and our practices. Nothing more."

"My father has rarely had interest in assisting another business unless it in some way will benefit him." Reid folded both arms over his chest. "If you truly have no inkling of Jackson Alexander playing your company like a fiddle in order to get to me through the ranch then you clearly *do* need help tightening your practices."

"However, if you do know Alexander is scheming and playing dirty, I will be sure your business is run so far under, you'll never see the light of day." Walker stood.

"And just in case it wasn't clear," Reid spoke as he stood to join Walker, "the Pine Ridge is *not* for sale and will *not* be available to Northern Plains Geothermal for acquiring the geothermal pocket."

"Have a nice day, Mr. Stewart." Walker nodded.

"And take it from someone who has known my father a lot longer than you have," Reid's steely words were quiet and serious, "he is not on your team, he isn't helping you, and he's simply using you." Reid gave a little wave and followed Walker out the door.

In the hallway, Walker took Reid's hand. "You were amazing in there."

Reid squeezed Walker's hand. "You weren't too shabby yourself."

The men nodded and offered polite waves to Charlene as they left and headed out of the building.

"Do you think Stewart knows my father is a slime ball?"

Walker shrugged. "My gut says Stewart knows Alexander is a shrewd businessman likely to go to extremes to get what he wants, but I don't think he knows what Alexander is up to with Pine Ridge."

"My guess is Daddy Dearest is strong-arming Northern Plains Geothermal into doing his bidding and being his front for getting the ranch back. I doubt Stewart or the company would allow themselves to get mixed up with anything unsavory if they knew about it going in." Reid frowned. "But knowing my father, he presents himself to them as the fine, upstanding businessman just looking out for their business in a way to increase his own."

"Yeah, your dad sure didn't turn out anything like his father." Walker bumped his shoulder against Reid's as they reached the hotel. "Luckily, you got all Grandpa Jack's good qualities and then some."

"Then some? What extra qualities did I get that

Grandpa Jack didn't possess?" Reid quickly pulled Walker into the elevator and pressed their floor number.

"If I remember your words correctly, you 'take dick in the ass and enjoy it. Immensely.'" Walker pressed Reid into a corner and rolled their hips together. "And I find that to be an extremely important quality in a man," Walker teased before capturing Reid's lips in a sensuous kiss.

"Lucky you," Reid murmured against Walker's lips.

"Lucky me," Walker agreed.

"Lucky me," Reid mumbled and moaned into the kiss.

"Lucky you." Walker chuckled as he broke the kiss just as the elevator car stopped.

## 15

"This is Reid Alexander." Walker put his arm around Reid as he smiled at his beloved Grandma. "Reid, this is my Grandma Rachel."

The short, slightly round, silver-haired woman beamed at her grandson before turning her attention to Reid.

"It's a pleasure to meet you." Reid stuck out his hand.

Rachel smacked his hand away and pulled him into a hug. "I knew this day would come, and I'm so very happy to finally meet you. No handshakes here, hugs all around." She reached out and pulled her grandson into the embrace.

Walker chuckled. "Knew this day would come? *Finally* meet him?" He pulled away from the hug. "I've not even known him for that long. It's not like you've been waiting years."

Rachel cocked a brow and patted his cheek. "You don't know that." She winked. "Plus, Norma has possibly been keeping me in the loop since I didn't know when *you* would finally bring this sweet man to meet me."

"Norma, of course." Walker shook his head.

Reid beamed and looped an arm around Walker's shoulders. "What can I say? The older ladies love me."

"Watch it, boy." Rachel poked him.

"Of course, by older I mean beautiful, wise, and mature," Reid replied with an impish grin.

"You boys are staying, right?" Rachel gestured toward her tiny living room.

"Thought we'd stay until this evening." Walker lowered onto the couch and patted the seat next to him.

Rachel frowned. "Only until evening? I guess I'll take what I can get, but I'd love you to visit longer than a few hours." She settled herself into a recliner.

"You have one bedroom, a small sofa, and hardwood floors," Walker replied. "We'll stay today, but I'd rather sleep in comfort."

Rachel pursed her lips. "Mmmhmm, *sleep* in *comfort*. I'll just bet that's why you want to be at a hotel."

Reid snorted.

Walker shot him a look.

Reid shrugged.

Rachel laughed.

"So what brings you boys to visit an old lady?" Rachel rocked gently in her chair.

"Stop," Walker groaned. "You act like I wasn't just here a few weeks ago."

"Were you?" Rachel shrugged. "Old people forget things so easily."

"Oh my Lord, pouring it on thick today are we?" Walker teased. "You weren't even forty when I was born. You're what, in your sixties? Hardly ancient." Walker shook his head. "We came to visit because we had to come to town to meet with Northern Plains Geothermal in regards to the ranch."

Rachel wrinkled her nose. "I thought Jack had already told them no about selling?"

"He did and I did, but they're back to sniffing around," Walker explained.

"My father didn't inherit my grandfather's morals," Reid chimed in. "Daddy Jack is pissed, pardon my language, because Grandpa Jack gave the ranch to me."

Rachel waved a hand. "Boy, there's no reason to apologize for language here. I'm the queen of F-bombs when they are called for." She frowned. "What does your father have to do with Northern Plains?"

"Well, according to the company, he's only a generous supporter and benefactor," Walker stated.

"But?" Rachel asked.

"Isn't there always a but?" Reid smiled. "It's too much of a coincidence that I inherited the ranch, the company is bugging us to buy again, my dad recently became part of their business in whatever way, *and* two cows were slaughtered at the edge of the property."

Rachel's hand covered her chest as she gasped. "No," she whispered. "Is your father really that evil?"

"He's definitely more closely related to the devil than an angel," Reid mumbled.

"I don't think Daddy Jack did the actual dirty work of killing the animals, but I'm certain he's behind it in some way," Walker said.

"Same with the geothermal company," Reid offered. "I doubt they know he's playing them, but I'm sure he is."

"Well, your dad just gained a hater." Rachel jutted her chin. "There's no reason to act like an ass just because your late father knew you couldn't be trusted to keep his ranch running."

"Daddy Jack cares about nothing but himself, his business, and his money." Reid rolled his eyes. "He wants to sell Pine Ridge to the very highest bidder and never look back. Bonus points if the buyer were to destroy the ranch land."

Rachel waved a hand. "Let's move on to happier topics." She rose from her chair and headed to the kitchen. "Would you boys like some lunch?"

"Let's go out," Walker suggested. "Or order in. No reason for you to cook."

"Who said *I* was going to cook?" Rachel winked. "But, I like that idea. We'll order in, you can go pick up the food, and Reid can keep me company."

"Oh Lord," Walker groaned.

"What?" Rachel batted her lashes in feigned innocence.

Walker rolled his eyes. "Nothing." He chuckled. "What do we want to eat?"

"I know you'd never look at this town and think it has a Chinese restaurant, but Mr. and Mrs. Zhang moved here several years ago with their children and have the market cornered on authentic Chinese food." Rachel nodded. "I swear, it's better than anything I've had in big cities."

Reid moaned and rubbed his stomach. "Oh my God, don't get me wrong, Norma is an amazing cook and I *love* her food. But I haven't had Chinese food since California and it sounds fabulous."

After placing an order that likely could have fed an entire football team, Walker grabbed his keys. He planted a kiss on Reid's lips and pointed at his grandmother. "You two behave," he ordered before walking out the door.

"Let's dish," Rachel exclaimed as she clasped her hands in front of her chest.

Reid laughed and pulled out a chair and sat at the

kitchen table. "Well, let's get to chatting. If I know Walker, he's going to drive like a bat out of hell to get back here before we have too much time to talk."

Rachel smiled and took a seat at the table. "You know him well." She cocked her head. "You love him, and he's head-over-heels in love with you." It was a statement, not a question.

Reid blushed and nodded. "Never even saw it coming. I came to South Dakota to serve out Grandpa Jack's required three months on the ranch, sell it, and move on."

Rachel leaned forward for the story, resting her elbows on the table.

"Hell, I was so focused on myself, getting rid of the ranch, and returning to California that I didn't even realize Walker was gay until he told me." He laughed. "I thought he was a straight guy looking to get in on some action, and I told him I wasn't down with being an experiment."

Rachel covered her laughter with a hand.

"He's an amazing man. You did a great job raising him," Reid stated.

Rachel's eyes softened. "Thank you. I hate that he grew up without his parents, but they weren't fit to raise a child."

"He was lucky to have you," Reid argued. "I know about being raised around a person not fit to be a parent. My father didn't have a lot to do with me, but he still affected me. Luckily, I think I grew up learning that I wanted to be *nothing* like him."

"I was able to meet your grandfather once before his passing," Rachel said. "He was a fine man. I can't thank him enough for bringing you into my Walker's life."

Reid cocked his head. "Do you think he *knew* Walker and I would hit it off? Like he orchestrated the whole thing?"

Rachel shrugged. "Who knows? I think he likely knew your father was definitely not going to keep the ranch. You were his choice because he knew if you could get to know the ranch you would maybe love it the way he did. You and Walker meeting and falling in love was icing on the cake." Rachel reached out and patted Reid's arm. "I know you never met him, but your grandpa was so very proud of you. And I'm pretty sure he thought of Walker as the son he never had. He'd be so thrilled you two are together and continuing the legacy of Pine Ridge."

"Did you ever meet Samuel?" Reid hated to bring up a sad subject, but his curiosity got the best of him.

Rachel nodded. "I did."

"You don't have to tell me anything about him," Reid added quickly. "I just feel bad sometimes, like I came to the ranch and took Samuel's place."

"Don't think that way," Rachel scolded. "Samuel was gone long before you arrived." She paused for a moment before continuing. "Sam was a nice man.

Good worker, reliable, loyal. He and Walker found a safe love with each other. I was grateful to know Walker had found someone. But as much as I truly believe they loved each other, I never saw my grandson's eyes sparkle the way they do when they look at you."

Reid's eyes stung. "I'm not looking for proof he loves me more, I promise I'm not."

"Baby, it's not a contest. He loved Samuel and he loves you. But his love for you is different. He wasn't unhappy with Sam, but he's beyond happy with you. You've brought a smile back to his face that I haven't seen since he was a small boy." Rachel wiped a tear. "For that and many other reasons, I absolutely adore you and have to say thank you for just being you."

Reid sniffed. "Well, this falling in love thing, like for real falling in love, has hit me like a bulldozer. But I can promise I love him with all of my heart, and I have no plans to live my life without Walker in it."

Rachel leaned forward and whispered, "Want to see baby pictures of him before he gets back?"

"Oh my God, woman." Reid laughed. "Of course!"

Rachel scurried out of the room and returned with two albums. "I grabbed one with baby years and one with teen years."

"Perfect," Reid said.

By the time Walker returned with lunch, Reid and Rachel had laughed and admired pictures of Walker's baby butt, first teeth, triumphant first steps, drooly smiles, and many more.

"Please tell me those aren't photo albums." Walker set bags on the kitchen counter.

"Oh, but they are," Reid teased. "No worries, you're in time for the teen years one."

Walker groaned. "I hate you both."

Reid popped up from the table and wrapped Walker in a hug. "No, you don't." He nibbled at Walker's neck. "You love us."

"Maybe," Walker grumped, but laughed as Reid continued to bite at his neck. "Fine, fine, I love you both."

"Food first, photos later," Rachel declared. "I'm starving, and I don't need soy sauce on my precious albums."

"Would you ever consider moving to the ranch?" Walker asked.

Rachel paused, a bite of fried rice in front of her mouth, and cocked her head. "Seriously?"

Walker shrugged. "I know you like your independence, and I'd never make you move there if you didn't want to, but I'd love to have you closer. You'd have Norma, the rest of the employees, the children, the animals."

"I'd pack my bags today if that's what you want," Rachel interrupted.

Walker smiled. "I thought you were going to argue with me."

"Nah, I love the Zhang's and their restaurant, I have a few friends here, but nothing's really holding me here." Rachel nodded as if she were considering the option even more. "Yeah, I think moving to the ranch would be wonderful." She pointed a chopstick at Walker. "But only if you really want me there, not because you think I *need* to be there."

"He really wants you there," Reid assured her. "He's been talking about asking you to move to Pine Ridge for a while."

"But I don't want you there until we figure out what's going on with the animals being killed," Walker interjected. "It may have been totally random, but I don't want to move you there if there's any danger. So, make your plans and get ready, but I'll keep you updated on the exact date."

"Sounds like a plan," Rachel agreed and smiled broadly. "I'm actually very excited about this prospect."

"We are too," Reid offered. "It will be great to have you there. Norma will adore having someone closer to her age. You'll love the kids. Perfect plan all around."

"We've got a couple hours before we need to head out." Walker glanced at the clock on the microwave. "You guys want to take a walk? Play a game? Watch a movie?"

"Awww, that's so cute," Rachel cooed and patted her grandson's hand.

"He thinks he can divert our attention from the photo albums," Reid stage whispered.

Walker rolled his eyes and huffed. "Fine, let's look at the damn pictures."

An hour later, the three of them had poured through most of the album. Rachel had paused to tell stories about certain pictures. Reid had interrupted with questions. And Walker had shared memories as they laughed at his hair styles and fashion choices.

"You were an adorable baby, but I love the gawky, nerdy teen trying to find himself," Reid stated and bumped his shoulder against Walker's. "And I'm glad you decided on the cowboy look because you're absolutely stunning in it." He leaned in to whisper, "Edible."

Rachel snorted. "I'm not sure whether to get googly eyes and say, 'awwww,' or grab a trashcan so I can upchuck." She shook her head. "You two are gorgeous, so cute, and absolute dears. But you're also sickeningly sweet."

"Sorry," Walker mumbled and blushed.

"Small price to pay," Reid teased with a shrug.

"I think you're blessed," Rachel said. "Very few people find the happiness you two seem to have found." She smiled. "Don't take it for granted."

"Blessed," Walker repeated the word as if testing it on his tongue. He nodded. "Yeah, blessed seems to fit."

Reid beamed before planting a sloppy kiss on Walker's cheek. "I agree. Blessed is perfect."

The evening wound down with coffee and pie before Reid and Walker headed back to the hotel.

"Well, I was dreading you leaving," Rachel quipped as she began to gather mugs and plates.

"Sit," Reid interrupted and jumped up to collect the dishes.

Rachel smirked. "Why thank you, child." She winked at Walker. "Like I said, I was dreading you leaving because I knew I'd be lonely and sad waiting on you to visit again. But now I'm ready to kick you out so I can start planning my move."

"Remember, not because I don't want you there, but wait for my word so I can rest easy knowing you're coming when it's safe," Walker reminded.

"All the better reason to kick you out so you can get back to the ranch and sort it all out." Rachel's eyes sparkled. "I need to give notice on this place, get boxes, inform doctors, inquire about another branch at my bank...oh my, there's just so much to do." She clasped her hands. "You two have made an old woman very happy."

"Old, right," Reid scoffed before pulling her into a hug. "Text or call if you want to make plans or have questions. You, Norma, and I should set up weekly lunch dates or something."

"Perfect," Rachel returned his hug before turning to

embrace Walker. "Be careful, you hear? Don't try to be the hero. I know you love that ranch, but you and the humans working and living there are a thousand times more important than the land or animals. Remember that."

"Will do." Walker hugged her tight. "Let me know if you need help with anything here. I can come over or find someone to help."

Rachel whispered, "He's amazing, I love him, and I love you. Seeing you happy makes my heart happy."

Reid took his leave and walked to the door. "I'll be in the car." He left Walker in his grandmother's arms.

"I love him so damn much," Walker choked out. "I don't even know how it happened. I wasn't even looking, had no plans to love someone again. He wasn't even pursuing me, didn't even know I was gay. It all just hit so suddenly." He shuddered. "I tried like hell to fight it, but my heart wouldn't let go."

"Our plans are nothing when it comes to love and what the heart wants." Rachel kissed his cheek and wiped away a tear. "Love him, be happy, and live your life. Be blessed."

"Thanks," Walker said. "Love you and see you soon."

"Drive safe," Rachel ordered as he walked to the door.

"Lock up behind me," Walker commanded.

"Always." Rachel gave him a little shove out the

door and turned the deadbolt before watching out the window as they drove away.

"I LOVE YOUR GRANDMA," Reid whispered as he crawled completely naked into the hotel bed and straddled an equally naked Walker, "but I love you even more." Quickly slicking himself with lube from the bedside table, Reid reached behind himself, grasped Walker's throbbing length, and pressed the head against his hole.

"Funny," Walker gritted out as Reid's tight heat engulfed him, "I love her too, but I love you even more. Or at least differently." His breath caught on a grunt as he rocked his hips and slid the rest of the way into Reid's ass. Walker gripped Reid's hips and held tight as Reid rode him slowly and sensually. "God, I love to watch you ride my dick. Come for me," Walker commanded.

Reid grasped his cock and jacked himself in rhythm to his ass on Walker's length. When Walker's speed increased, Reid stroked himself faster until he moaned and painted his release all over Walker's chest before collapsing, letting Walker piston hard and fast until Walker roared and filled Reid's ass with his load.

## 16

"Yes?" Walker's gruff voice rumbled into the phone as he roused from sleep the next morning.

"Boss, we got a problem," Wes answered.

Reid rolled over to listen to the conversation as Walker flipped the phone to speaker.

"Figured as much since you're calling so early." Walker sat up. "What's the problem?"

"One of the horses has gone down," Wes replied. "Vet's here, sitting with the animal now. He thinks it may be poisoning of some sort."

Walker and Reid shot from the bed and began throwing their belongings into bags as the conversation continued.

"Which horse?" Reid asked as he pulled a shirt over his head.

"Buttercup," Wes stated.

Reid and Walker shared a distraught glance.

Reid accepted the soft hand on his shoulder and dropped his chin to his chest.

"We'll be on the road within thirty minutes," Walker advised. "Keep us updated if the situation changes." Walker disconnected the call and tossed the phone onto the bed. "Fuck," he whispered into the silence of the room.

"How often does a horse recover from a poisoning?" Reid asked with a frown as he finished dressing, packing, and then headed to the bathroom.

"When a big animal goes down, it's hard to get it back up. Injury to a horse is near lethal at times." Walker shook his head. "Don't know about poisoning. Never had an animal poisoned, but I'd have to venture the outcome isn't great."

"I thought as much," Reid murmured and pinched the bridge of his nose.

The men loaded the truck and headed toward Pine Ridge.

"You want to stop for food?" Walker asked.

"No, not even hungry," Reid answered quickly. "Just want to get home and see Buttercup."

Walker reached for Reid's hand. "Babe, I know you bonded with Buttercup, but you probably should prepare for the worst in this situation."

Reid sighed. "I know. I just want to be with her."

They were silent for several miles.

"God damn it, this is all my fault," Reid muttered as he bounced a fist off the window.

Walker shot a look his way. "Whoa, how do you figure that?"

"If I'd refused the ranch, sold it to my dad, sold it to *anyone*, none of this would be happening." Reid ran a hand over his face.

"Stop," Walker commanded. "Don't think that for even a second more. I don't think you had the option of refusing the ranch based on Jack's wishes in his will. Selling to your father would have guaranteed the death, literally and figuratively, of most of the animals and employees. Selling to anyone else would have had the same outcome. You staying on at the ranch likely gave the whole place and all the people the best chance at making it through the loss of our beloved owner. So stop that blame shit right now."

Reid gritted his teeth and leaned forward, head in hands. "I'm just so fucking mad. My dad is not a good person, but I never thought he'd stoop to killing animals to get his way." He moved his hands to grip fistfuls of his hair. "The fact that he likely *knows* he's hurting me in the process is just the icing on the cake."

"I'm sorry," Walker offered. "What's happening sucks, but it's not your fault, and I'm glad to have you by my side through it."

They arrived at the ranch and met a barn full of concerned faces.

Norma hugged them both and Wes stepped forward.

"Doc thinks Buttercup got into some wilted Red Maple leaves," Wes explained.

"Not possible, all the Red Maple trees on the property were cut down." Walker shook his head. "We keep an eye out to make sure that type of tree doesn't grow where the horses can get to the leaves, wilted or not."

Wes nodded. "I agree." He glanced toward the area where the vet was set up to diagnose, observe, and assist Buttercup. "We all know wilted Red Maple leaves are extremely toxic to horses, but there aren't any around here, so where did it come from? Buttercup was lethargic, pale yellow gums, refused to eat, breathing heavy. I didn't know what was up, but Doc ran through the list of signs and symptoms and it fits Red Maple."

"What's the prognosis?" Reid crossed his arms over his chest.

"Doc said as little as a pound or two of the leaves can be fatal, but he's not sure if the animal ingested that much," Wes explained. "He's started intravenous fluids. Blood transfusion isn't out of the question, but not for sure right now. Doc says we likely got treatment early enough Buttercup *could* survive."

"Where did she pasture last?" Walker asked.

"That's just it, Boss," Wes continued. "She didn't go

out to pasture. I rode her to check the fence line one day, definitely no Red Maple. Took her out to round up some of the cattle another day. And yesterday we exercised her in the arena before a storm rolled in. She's not been out to pasture in at least three days."

"So that means someone fed her the leaves," Reid concluded.

"Seems like it," Wes agreed.

"Call the police. I want them here for statements, photographs, everything." Walker reached for Reid's hand. "Let's talk to Doc, see what he knows right now."

Doctor Litel didn't have much more to tell the men than what Wes had shared. "I am pretty sure we caught it early enough that she could pull through. Pretty much a wait and see right now. She won't be out of the woods for a day or so. We'll keep the fluids running and have blood on standby if needed."

"Will she recover completely if she lives?" Reid asked.

"Really no way of knowing that," Doc shrugged and ran a hand over Buttercup's nose as they both sat on the floor. "She's a strong animal, so she has that going for her."

"Tell us what to watch for," Walker commanded, "then go grab some food at the house. Norma will fix you up."

"Gentlemen, my legs are so fast asleep I will definitely take you up on that." Doc Litel scribbled down some numbers on a chart before unfolding himself from the barn floor. "If her heartrate goes up or down more than five to ten points, get me back in here. If she gets agitated or looks like she's seizing, give me a call. Other than that, she's got about two hours left on that fluid before I'll start more. I'll be back in a bit. Gonna eat, make some calls, and do a little more research into Red Maple."

"Don't leave without speaking to the police," Walker told Doc. "Wes is calling them. I want this all reported. Along with the two cattle found with their throats cut. We reported that incident, as well, but I want to make sure it's all connected in the reports."

Reid gently lowered himself to the floor, talking quietly to Buttercup. "Hey, baby girl," he cooed as he softly rubbed her velvety nose. "I'm so sorry, sweet girl."

Buttercup snorted softly and nudged Reid's hand. By the time Walker joined them on the barn floor, Reid had maneuvered himself so that Buttercup's head was on his lap.

"That can't be comfortable," Walker murmured.

Reid shrugged. "She's uncomfortable thanks to my dad, least I can do is let her lean on me."

"Well, here, let me sit behind you so you can rest on me," Walker ordered as he moved behind Reid.

When the men and their horse were situated, all three gave a somewhat contented sigh.

"Look at you," Walker teased. "You were scared to

death of horses when you first came here and now you're snuggling with one."

Reid chuckled. "Okay, so not *all* horses are evil. Cinnamon and Buttercup are my girls."

"Are those the only ones?"

"The jury is still out on that," Reid replied. "The bigger and more fierce a horse looks, the more likely I am to be scared to death of them."

"We'll keep working on it." Walker nuzzled his nose again Reid's ear. "No ranch owner, boyfriend, or partner of mine is going to be scared of horses."

Reid snorted. "Whatever. We'll see."

"You'll see, I'm right," Walker claimed. "You wouldn't even walk in the barn not long ago. You're making massive progress. I'll convince you that horses are kind and gentle if you just give them the chance."

They were silent for several moments, seemingly lost in thought.

"What's your read on Doc? Seems that he's worried, but has hope." Reid lay back on Walker's chest, but his hand didn't stop gently rubbing Buttercup's snout and neck.

"I agree." Walker kissed the side of Reid's head. "I don't get the feeling Doc thinks she's completely out of the woods, but he seems sure that it was caught early enough that she *could* recover completely, or at least survive."

"Don't get me wrong, I want her to survive," Reid

whispered, "but what type of life does a horse have if they aren't completely recovered?"

"We'd make sure she's comfortable." Walker rubbed Reid's arm. "Whatever level of recovery she reaches, we'll make sure she feels needed and reaches her potential. She'll have a good life no matter what."

Reid was quiet for a moment. "That's one of the reasons I love you, you're so very good all the way to your core." He turned his head and looked up at Walker. "Animals, people, they're all so lucky to know you." He used his free hand to pull Walker's lips close to his before whispering, "And I'm the luckiest of all to call you mine."

"Always and forever," Walker murmured, his lips touching Reid's gently.

When the kiss dissolved, Reid asked, "Will the police take this seriously?"

"Yes, without a doubt," Walker assured him. "There's not a ton of crime around here, so they'll be very interested for one. Plus, I've got several friends on the force. And I'm friends with a lot of very influential people in town. No one will be okay with this. We stick together around here. Doc Phips is probably already organizing an angry mob."

"I hope they can catch the person or people responsible quickly." Reid shuddered. "I can't stand the thought of more animals being hurt. Or what if they move to hurting people?"

"Exactly. That's why we have to up the security until we get to the bottom of this." Walker wrapped an arm around Reid's chest. "I won't stand for my animals or people to be endangered or hurt."

The police and Dr. Litel found the men and the horse asleep an hour later.

"Looks like resting with the two of you is good medicine," Dr. Litel stated as he checked Buttercup's vitals. "Her numbers are better than they were when I left her."

Reid and Walker switched places with the doctor so they could give their statements to the police.

Thirty minutes later, Officer Toweler closed his notebook. "Thanks, gentlemen. We'll get the S.O.B., I can promise you that. The type of people that would do these things are usually acting on the part of someone higher up. Once we find the ones responsible for the actual crimes, all we have to do is work our magic to get them to blab. They always do. We just have to find the right key."

"Thanks, Mark," Walker thanked the officer and shook his hand.

"Thank you," Reid copied the action. "I'm one hundred percent sure you'll end up tracing this whole thing to my father, so whatever needs to be done to keep an eye on him I'd say do it."

"We don't have the jurisdiction to do anything from here without concrete evidence that he's involved, but

I'll call the departments around where he lives and does most of his work, just so they can have him on their radar." Officer Toweler tipped his hat and gave a wave to the other officers to take their leave. "Best wishes on your animal, Corrigan. Shameful to see such a gorgeous horse brought down."

Once the officer left, Walker and Reid checked on Buttercup once again.

"Go have some food before Norma sends out a search party for you," Dr. Litel told them.

They all laughed. Even Buttercup snorted as if she knew the truth behind the statement.

"Will do." Walker nodded. "We'll be back in a bit. You can go home after. We'll stay with her overnight."

"Sounds good." Dr. Litel prepared more IV fluids for Buttercup. "I'll start this one and show you how to switch it out before I leave. I'll be available through the night if needed. I'll come check on her tomorrow morning. If her numbers look this good or better by then I think she's got a really good chance of pulling through."

Walker followed Reid to the house for food. "Damn, I didn't realize how hungry I am until just now."

"Same," Reid agreed. "I wasn't at all hungry when we left this morning or when we were in the barn, but now I'm starving."

Norma met them at the door. "I hope you're hungry. I've been worried, and I cook when I'm worried. I've made six pies, a cake, and a week's worth of food."

Walker and Reid laughed and snuggled Norma between them as they walked to the kitchen.

"I can likely eat at least one of everything right now." Reid rubbed his hands together and glanced around the room. "Holy shit, lady, you weren't kidding. This place looks like a professional kitchen preparing for a party of five hundred."

Norma shrugged. "Better than smoking or drugs or other negative habits when I'm nervous."

The three sat down to visit and eat.

"You two should rest for an hour or so before you go back to the barn," Norma suggested. "Doctor Litel said he could stay until evening, so take a nap before he leaves."

Reid and Walker glanced at each other and nodded.

"That actually sounds like a great idea," Walker said.

"Agreed," Reid stated. "Now that I'm not so hungry, I realize how tired I am."

## 17

The next morning, Reid sighed in relief when Doc Litel declared Buttercup wasn't one hundred percent out of the woods, but she was well on her way to a full recovery. *You're getting teary eyed over a horse? Will wonders never cease?*

"We'll need to keep her hydrated and fed," Doc said. "She should probably stay down and rest today if you can keep her down."

"Have you ever tried to keep a horse down if they want to get up?" Walker snorted.

"If she's wanting to get up, let her." Doc smiled and winked. "She'll know if she's feeling up to it."

"Keep her in the barn today or walk her if she gets herself up?" Reid asked.

"If she's up, I'd walk her, but only a couple laps in the arena and no faster than a slow human walk. She will likely wear down easier. Have lots of water and food readily available." Doc ran a hand down Buttercup's neck. "If she gets up today and does okay with a short, slow walk, you can do the same tomorrow. I wouldn't add more walking for a couple days. But, if she shows she's wanting to go longer or faster, let her."

"Sounds good, Doc." Walker shook the doctor's hand. "Can't tell you how much we appreciate you being here and getting her through this."

"I'm grateful I was able to help." Doctor Litel nodded. "Wes and the others did a good job of catching the signs early, probably made all the difference."

Walker and Reid accompanied Doc to his truck.

"I'll check in throughout the day and over the next week," Dr. Litel informed them.

"Appreciate it." Walker nodded. "We'll keep you updated. Won't let her be alone for the next day or so."

Doc Litel waved as he drove off.

Walker threw an arm around Reid as they walked back to the barn.

"Wow, this could have ended so much differently," Reid sighed and snuggled into Walker's side. "I know the whole thing isn't over, but I'm so glad she's going to be okay."

"Yeah, me too," Walker agreed. "Now we just need to get to the bottom of it all before any other animals or people get hurt."

"SHE GOT UP LAST NIGHT," Wes rubbed Buttercup's neck. "Figured you could walk her today, see how she does."

"Sounds good," Walker replied. "Take a couple hours off before you work with the new mare. I've got Zeke and Dusty running errands today. Reid and I will stick around the barn and keep an eye on things."

"Will do, boss." Wes tipped his hat before leaving the barn.

"Hey, sweet girl, you ready to take a walk?" Reid let Buttercup nuzzle his chest.

Walker and Reid led the animal from the barn and began a very slow pace around the ring. Buttercup made no effort to speed up, so the men kept to a slow walk.

"Sure took a lot out of her," Walker stated he ran his gaze over the horse, "but looks like she's up to getting through it. We will all take turns walking her until she's got her strength up. Maybe keep someone on duty in the barn through the night."

"Let her take it slow for a few days. I bet she's back to herself within a week." Reid patted Buttercup's neck.

Zeke waved from the fence and gave a whistle.

Walker headed to see what the kid wanted. After a few moments of conversation, Walker returned to Reid and Buttercup.

"I'm going to ride out to check the western

perimeter fence." Walker adjusted his hat. "Shouldn't
be more than an hour. If there's damage, I'll fix it best I
can. May have to take more supplies out to finish it
tomorrow."

"Is there a problem?" Reid frowned.

"Zeke said a neighbor noticed a breach in the fence."
Walker shrugged.

"One, it kills me when you say *neighbor* because the
closest people are like ten miles away." Reid started
listing points with his fingers. "Two, who is this neighbor? Three, why can't he fix it?"

Walker chuckled. "One, it's more like two or three
miles in any direction for the most part. Two, it's Old
Man Sullivan. Three, again, it's Old Man Sullivan. He's
not in any position to mend fences. His property is
small, and he doesn't make much of a profit. He can't
hire men to do the work for him, so I help out as much as
possible."

Reid leaned in and kissed him. "You're too good."
With one hand holding Buttercup's reins and the
other hand on Walker's shoulder, Reid continued,
"But can't you send someone else or let me go with
you?"

Walker shook his head. "Not really. I've got all the
others doing errands or chores. You're welcome to come
with me, but Buttercup is the only horse you've ever
ridden. You'd be fine on any, you were a quick learner,
and the terrain isn't bad to the west."

Reid grimaced. "Well, when you put it that way, I'm just going to have to trust you'll be okay."

Walker laughed. "I see how it is," he teased as he hooked a thumb in Reid's beltloop and pulled him close for a kiss. "I won't be long. Let her walk a couple more laps, then give her plenty of water and food before giving her a good rub down."

"I'll spend some time with Cinnamon, too," Reid offered. "I can't wait until that girl is big enough for me to ride."

Buttercup neighed and blew a breath against Reid's back before pushing him gently with her snout.

Walker and Reid laughed at her clear message.

"Calm down, baby. You'll always be my first," Reid cooed at her neck.

Walker saddled up one of the other horses and rode off to the west.

Reid finished up with Buttercup and left her to rest in her stall with fresh water, feed, and hay. He found Cinnamon out in the pasture and whistled for her to come to the fence. The filly's ears perked, and she pranced toward Reid, flipping her mane and shaking her head.

"Hey girl, hey there pretty girl," Reid murmured as the horse nuzzled his hand. "Want to go walk?" He unlatched the gate. Reid held onto Cinnamon's halter until they reached the ring and he could put a lead on her.

Twenty minutes later, Cinnamon's feistiness was waning, and Reid debated whether to return her to the pasture or the stable. Leaving the ring, Cinnamon turned to the pasture, so the decision was made.

Reid followed the filly into the pasture and patted her. "Okay girl, I'll come visit again tomorrow."

As he unhooked the lead, he heard a deafening *crack* split the air and echoed across the ranch.

Cinnamon bolted.

Reid flinched. Turning to the west where the sound seemed to originate, Reid's stomach sank. "Fuck, that was a gunshot, wasn't it?" he asked the emptiness around him as he steadied himself against the fence.

A million thoughts raced through his head. *Is there a four-wheeler available? How much time would it take to go look? But if there's no vehicle available, that's just a waste of time. Should I walk toward the shot? Wait for Wes or Zeke or somebody? Saddle up another horse?*

*Oh hell, no. I can't ride another horse.*

At that moment, thundering hooves sounded behind him, and Reid fearfully ducked his head to protect himself from what he knew was a charging horse.

But the sound stopped right at his back and only the heavy breathing of the animal was heard. Reid turned slowly and came face-to-face with the giant Beauty. She nudged him with her nose, pressing against his chest as she pawed the ground and whinnied.

"Seriously?" Reid sighed. "Okay, let's go." He had to

extend his arm to take hold of Beauty's halter, but the horse took the lead and headed to the stable.

When they entered the darkness of the barn, Reid's eyes struggled to adjust, but he immediately recognized the voice.

"That sounded like a gun shot," Norma stated. "I rushed down here as quickly as I could."

"Walker went to check the west perimeter fence," Reid informed her. "This beast basically came to me and demanded I ride her out to see what happened. Can you help me saddle her up?"

Within five minutes, Norma and Reid had Beauty ready to ride.

Norma slid a step stool next to the massive animal and held the reins as Reid climbed on. Beauty stood stock still as if she knew the importance of being calm and gentle at a scary and unsure moment.

"You head on out, I'll call some of the others and tell them what happened. They won't be far behind." Norma patted Reid's leg and Beauty's neck. "God speed." She turned and headed to the barn office.

Reid clicked his tongue and signaled Beauty gently with his boots as Walker had shown him, and the horse left the barn.

Beauty moved quickly from a trot to a canter to a smooth gallop as Reid's head and heart imagined the unimaginable that lay before him.

❀

"Whoa," Reid pulled back on Beauty's reins as they came close to the west end fence. "Shit, he could be anywhere," Reid whispered to the wide-open quietness and patted Beauty's neck. "You were amazing, girl. Smoothest ride ever. Don't tell Buttercup I said that. I'll deny it."

"If you're done chatting with the horse, I'd take a little help over here," Walker's voice sounded at Reid's back.

Whipping his head around and turning Beauty, Reid moved toward a large rock and found Walker sitting in the shade of the boulder with a handkerchief held against the back of this head.

"Shit!" Reid slid from the saddle. "Were you shot?"

"No," Walker answered. "The gunshot scared the shit out of Rascal. He reared up and threw me. I think I busted my head on a rock. Definitely gonna have some bruises on my back, felt like I landed on a gravel road."

"Let me see your head," Reid commanded.

Walker removed the cloth and winced. "Careful, it hurts like hell."

"There's a lot of blood." Reid took the handkerchief and whistled.

"Head wounds bleed a lot."

"Did you pass out?" Reid feathered a touch across Walker's head.

"No, I got Rascal tied up and then came here to sit in the shade." Walker shook his head. "My phone must have fallen off my holder. Figured if someone didn't show up pretty soon I'd pull myself up and look for it."

"Sorry it took me so long," Reid apologized and stood to help Walker stand. "Careful. Are you dizzy?"

Walker steadied himself against the rock and held his head. "Little bit, mostly just throbbing where it's bleeding."

Reid glanced around. "Let's wrap your head first. Think you can ride back?"

"Yeah, I'll be fine." Walker frowned as he glanced between Beauty and Reid. "Damn, I either hit my head a lot harder than I thought and I'm imagining things, or you really do love me."

Reid snorted. "I didn't really have a choice. Beauty pretty much charged me and demanded I ride her out here. Norma helped me saddle her up."

"Wow," Walker crooned. "Great ride, right?" He smirked.

"Amazing ride, barely felt it, like her legs were floating over the ground." Reid shook his head and adjusted his hat as he watched the beast of a horse graze a few feet away.

"I told you," Walker teased.

"I know, I know," Reid agreed, "but I'll tell you like I told Beauty, don't mention this to Buttercup. She can't know I cheated on her."

Walker chuckled and winced again. "Damn, that hurts. You got your phone?"

Reid nodded.

"Call Doc and see if she can come out and check my head. See if I need stitches." Walker ripped first one sleeve then another from his shirt. "Here, use this to tie that hanky to my head to slow the bleeding."

Reid took the cloth, made the call, and then gingerly affixed the cloth to Walker's head.

"I think we should both ride Beauty," Walker declared. "That way if I get woozy, I won't fall from Rascal, and you can hold me on."

"Good idea," Reid looked toward Rascal. "Leave him or lead him back?"

"Any other time, I'd leave him and let someone come out and get him." Walker frowned. "But I don't know if that gunshot was random or a warning or meant to spook the horse, so I don't want to leave him out here."

"Completely agree." Reid thumbed his phone screen. "I'm texting Wes and Norma to make sure the police know about this."

Reid collected Rascal from his place on the fence and brought him to the rock.

"You want to get on first or me?" Reid pointed to Beauty.

"I'll get on first, and then you climb on behind me."

Walker mounted Beauty and groaned at the exertion. "Fuck, that hurts."

"Dude, this is like the tallest horse I've ever seen," Reid grumbled as he stared up at Walker.

"Get your foot in the stirrup and then mount up. I'll grab your arm and help."

Within an hour, thanks to needing to go slowly and also lead Rascal, the quartet arrived back at the ranch. Wes and a few other ranch hands met Walker and Reid and took the horses while Doc immediately ushered Walker into the house. Reid paced as Doc patched up Walker and Norma made sure there was food for at least two football teams.

Two hours later, the horses were safely away for the night with an extra watch patrolling the ranch. Walker's head was patched up. Showers were taken and dinner was eaten.

"Dude, I'm so damn tired, I think I could sleep for a year," Walker moaned as he settled into bed, gasping as his wound hit the pillow.

"Well, Rip Van Winkle, you're going to hate me by morning," Reid teased.

Walker cocked a brow.

"Doc says I have to wake you every hour because you have a concussion."

Walker frowned. "Why didn't she tell *me* that?"

"Probably because she knew you'd pout and throw a hissy."

Walker started to answer, likely to argue, but he stopped. "Yeah, you're probably right." He pulled back the covers and patted the bed. "Let's get comfy and sleep an hour at a time."

"Ohhhh, sounds so romantic," Reid cooed.

## 18

"Walker, Reid, nice to see you," Officer Toweler spoke to the men as he shook their hands. "Wanted to come by and update you on what we know."

"Down," Walker commanded. He tried to stop the dogs from prancing around their visitor, but his head hurt too much to bend over.

"Have a seat," Walker offered. "Norma will bring coffee."

"No need to go to any trouble for me," the officer waved off the suggestion. He smiled as Donald jumped on his lap followed by Louise. The other three wiggled all over Toweler's boots.

"She likely started the coffee the moment she saw your car pull in," Reid said. "And I'd guess she'll have some sort of sweet to go with it. Trying to stop Norma from providing hospitality is like trying to stop the sun from rising." Reid sat and patted the cushion next to him and got Huey's attention. The dog darted from the officer to Reid's side.

Norma bustled into the living room. "Morning, Mark. I hope you've brought good news. I have coffee and cinnamon rolls."

"Morning, and that sounds wonderful." Officer Toweler nodded. "Thank you."

Norma sat the tray on the coffee table before taking a seat.

Around a mouth full of pastry Toweler said, "I think the extra patrols have likely kept more incidences from happening. My officers heard a bit of chatter about someone who may have a hand in all of it." Toweler took a sip of coffee. "They caught up with him just on the outskirts of town at a rundown campsite. We've taken him in because he was found with drugs, *and* he admitted to doing some of the things out here on the ranch. The fireworks during the party, the gun shot that spooked Walker's horse, he swears he wouldn't kill an animal and hasn't admitted to the cattle deaths or the poisoning."

"Who is he? Who is he working for?" Walker demanded.

"Trey Cox." Toweler shrugged. "We can't find any connection between him and Alexander at this point.

Cox swears he was doing odd jobs for someone in the next town over in exchange for drugs and money."

"Find that person and I bet you find a connection to my father," Reid grumbled. "Or at least it will be one step closer to finding the connection to him."

"We're on it." Toweler nodded. "My men are getting more information from Cox and looking for his contact. At this point, we have every reason to suspect Alexander is behind this whole thing. He's got motive, he's got the history of some unsavory actions, he's got the money and the connections to make it happen. But, we need strong evidence against him before we just go in guns blazing. Without evidence, he'll lawyer up and never have to answer for any of it."

"Even with evidence, he's going to lawyer up," Reid interrupted.

"But with evidence, we can at least charge him, right?" Walker asked.

"Exactly," Toweler answered. "I wish I had more to tell you, but for now I'll thank you kindly for the coffee and treat and be on my way. I'll update you when we have more information."

After a hug for Norma, Officer Toweler followed Walker and Reid outside.

A few more pleasantries were exchanged before the officer drove off.

Walker and Reid headed toward the barn and met Zeke on the way.

"Morning," Zeke mumbled.

"What's up?" Walker asked, frowning.

"Shay has a doctor appointment. Wes wants to do a date and overnight after, but Shay is insistent that I not be used as a babysitter." Zeke crossed his arms over his chest.

"She doesn't trust you with Elise?" Reid asked with eyebrows raised.

"Nah, she trusts me fine, she just has this thing about not using me as a babysitter, like taking advantage of me. I told her I don't care, but she's adamant," Zeke grumped.

"I think we can help," Walker offered with a wink.

"Yeah?" Zeke brightened.

"I'll pull the boss card. Tell them they have to take the night off. Reid and I will watch Elise. You'll be there to help if needed, but the two of us will be the babysitters." Walker smiled broadly.

"That may work." Zeke nodded. "Elise wants pizza, you guys okay with that? She also loves to watch Disney movies on repeat and sing the songs," he warned.

"Pizza and singing? Throw in dancing and I'm in my own personal heaven." Reid pretended to swoon. "I'm in."

"Sounds good. I'll talk to Wes and make it happen." Walker slapped Zeke on the back. "Guess we'll see you tonight."

Zeke smiled and waved as he walked off, clearly

happier than before.

"He's a good kid," Walker pondered aloud.

"Yeah, he is," Reid agreed. "Can I just say how excited I am for babysitting? Pizza, singing, and you know I'm going to teach Elise to dance. Maybe we bring the duck dogs with us? It's like a big ol' slumber party."

Walker groaned. "I hope I have the energy for what I just signed us up for."

"No worries, Cowboy, we've got this," Reid quipped and kissed Walker on the cheek. "Come on, let's go tell Wes the plan."

"WHAT THE HELL HAVE YOU DONE?" Reid growled into the phone as way of greeting.

"Afternoon, son. Nice to hear your voice," Jack Alexander crooned.

"Fuck off," Reid snapped. "You're fucking with *lives* here. Is a piece of land really worth killing animals and putting people in danger?"

"I'm sure I have no idea what you're going on about," Jack answered. "But I've called with an offer I think you'll find very profitable."

"I'm not interested."

"Hear me out," Jack continued.

Reid was silent.

"Sell the ranch to me. I'll make sure your little

boyfriend is able to find a job at another ranch. When I sell the property, I'll give you half." Jack paused for a moment. "That's enough money to do whatever you want. You and that faggot won't have a single moment of worry about money. You can do whatever you'd like with the money, and you won't have to hear from me ever again."

Reid pinched the bridge of his nose and clenched his jaw. "All of this because you're bent out of shape that Grandpa Jack gave me the ranch instead of you? I don't get it. What's in it for you?"

"I'm a business man. I know a good business deal when I see one. A ranch like that isn't going to be profitable forever. Best to sell now and move on." Jack's words were smooth. "And selling to me will net you at least ten percent more than any other buyer. As my son, I'm willing to share the profits with you when I sell the land."

"Grandpa Jack wanted Pine Ridge to stay in the family. This place was his life. He didn't give it to you because he knew you'd sell it." Reid paused and waited for his father's answer.

"My dad was good at what he did, but he wasn't a business man. He was a rancher through-and-through," Jack began. "He was too close to the ranch, and I fear you've developed too much of a sentimental attachment to it, as well. Let me do what I do best, and you'll never have to worry about money again."

"Pardon my lack of trust, *Father*," Reid sneered into the phone. "You've never in your life done anything out of the goodness of your heart, so this offer is sending up red flags left and right."

"You're going to regret it if you don't sell to me. When that ranch goes belly-up, you'll wish you had taken the deal," Jack growled.

"Is that a threat?"

"It's just the truth."

"I'll take my chances," Reid quipped. "You seem much too interested in this land. You're not wanting to keep it in the family. It's not going to net you a super high sale price even with the geothermal heat pocket. There's something else going on, I just can't figure it out yet. You've never offered such a generous deal to me, in fact, you've never offered *any* deal to me. Something's up."

"You've always been too dramatic for your own good," Jack huffed back at his son. "It's a good deal. If you don't take it now, you'll end up taking a massive cut when you have to sell a bankrupt and dead ranch in a few years."

"Again with the threats, I'll be sure to have the police add that in their notes," Reid shot back. "Thanks for the call, thanks for the offer, but 'it's a no from me, dawg,'" Reid purred into the phone. "And feel free to never contact me again."

After ending the call, Reid stood staring at the

phone screen for several moments. "What the hell? Why in the world is he so damn interested in this land?" Reid mumbled aloud to the nothingness around him.

"WHAT'S UP? YOU SEEM DISTRACTED," Walker asked as they and the five dogs walked from the main house to Wes and Shay's home just on the west side of the property.

The duck squad was busy sniffing every single plant, rock, and twig they could find while simultaneously marking their territory every three steps.

"My dad called today," Reid murmured.

"What?" Walker stopped in his tracks. "What did he say?"

Reid grabbed Walker's hand and pulled him along as he spoke. "Had a *deal* to offer me. Said he'd pay ten percent more for the ranch than any other buyer then he'd give me half the profits when he sells the land."

Walker was silent for a moment. "That's a really good deal. What did you tell him?"

Reid snorted. "Good deal? Maybe. But I don't trust him. He's up to something. Never once has he done anything *good* without an ulterior motive. And he's never offered any type of deal to me. I call bullshit. There's a reason he wants the ranch so badly."

"So you don't want the money?" Walker whispered.

"I mean, we all want money. But I told him to shove his deal up his ass." Reid squeezed Walker's hand as they neared Wes and Shay's. "And I told him I would tell the police about his call and thinly veiled threats, *plus* look into why he might be so determined to own Pine Ridge before selling it."

"What threats? What did he say?" Walker growled.

Reid shrugged as they waited for the dogs to catch up. "Just some remarks about how I'll regret not selling now when the ranch is belly-up and I have to take a massive cut in selling a bankrupt and dead ranch later."

Walker took a deep breath. "I'd like to think he's just blowing smoke, but he has the power to wreck us if we're being honest."

"Even if I wasn't in love with you and the ranch and the people, at this point I'm willing to call his bluff." Reid knelt down to pet Huey and Louise. "We're going to report the call and all the details to Toweler. Connect my dad to all of the shit going on at the ranch. And then figure out why he's so damn insistent on buying. He has no sentimental attachment to the land or the ranch; he's got something else going on, some other reason to be so interested." Reid stood and pulled Walker into a hug before kissing him softly. "And now we're going to spend an evening enjoying pizza, movies, singing, dancing, and babysitting."

Walker melted into Reid's kiss before pulling back and smiling. "Okay, sounds like a good plan."

AFTER SEVERAL HOURS OF PIZZA, ice cream, singing, dancing, giggles, and Elise doing hair and makeup on all three men, they finally marched her off to bed.

"Can the puppies sleep on my bed?" Elise yawned as she crawled into bed with all five dogs jumping up onto the bed and settling in.

"Sure," Reid answered with a wink.

Walker laughed. "It's a good thing you want them here, since I think they already had plans for where they wanted to sleep."

"Can we have another sleepover soon?" Elise's eyes were closed and her words were thick with sleep.

"Definitely," Walker whispered as he tucked her in. "Sleep tight, sweet girl."

The child was asleep with the duck dogs curled up around her before Reid and Walker even reached the hallway.

Zeke watched from the recliner as Walker and Reid settled on the couch and curled into each other.

"You guys must really like each other, huh?" Zeke cocked his head.

Reid snorted as he snuggled under Walker's arm. "What gave it away?"

Zeke smiled and shook his head. "It's just that you seem to not give a fuck what anyone thinks about who you're with."

Walker glanced down at Reid's upturned face and gave him a quick kiss. "I used to be. Used to worry I'd never get a job or have friends or be safe if anyone knew I liked men."

"What changed for you?" Zeke asked.

Walker shrugged. "No one specific event. I simply learned to love and value myself. I realized I had to be true to myself. I didn't want any job or friend that couldn't accept me as the real me."

"What about being safe? Don't you worry about gay bashing and shit like that?" Zeke leaned forward to put his elbows on his knees. "I can't even go anywhere without at least one comment about being mixed. A mixed gay kid? Isn't that just asking for it?"

"Can I ask you something?" Reid interjected quietly.

Zeke nodded.

"Are you trying to figure out if you're gay? Or are you trying to figure out whether or not you want to come out?" Reid fixed a stare on the younger man.

Zeke took a deep breath. "I'm gay." He shivered violently and held his head. "Wow, that's the first time I've said those words to anyone other than myself in the mirror."

"When did you know?" Reid asked.

"Middle school, I guess. All the guys were going on and on about boobs and short skirts, and all I could think about was the way a dick looked in sweats and what it would be like to be held in a guy's arms." Zeke sighed heavily. "I don't think I finally accepted it until you showed up and called me out."

"Sorry about that," Reid offered.

"Don't be." Zeke shook his head. "When you came here all out and proud it made me want to be that. Watching you two together made me think I could have that someday."

"You can." Walker nodded.

"I'm just not sure how to go about it," Zeke murmured.

"There's no right or wrong. No special timeline," Walker offered.

"I don't even know how to meet guys." Zeke threw himself against the back of the recliner. "Like some hot gay guy my age is just going to show up on a remote horse ranch in Soth Dakota and fall for me."

Walker and Reid looked at each other and busted out laughing.

"Never say never." Reid chuckled.

Zeke rolled his eyes. "Maybe I'll be lucky like you two. But until then, do I just sit around and beat off to gay porn?"

Walker and Reid exploded into laughter again.

"Nothing wrong with beating off to gay porn," Walker stated. "Some of the online dating apps may be helpful, but please check with us or take a friend if you're meeting someone. Meeting strangers can be scary and dangerous."

"We can check out some gay bars or at least gay-friendly bars if you'd like," Reid offered.

"Yeah, that would be good." Zeke nodded. "I'm not ready to just announce it to the world yet, so can you keep it quiet?"

"No worries. And you may never be ready to tell everyone. Sometimes it's easier to tell a few people at a time and work your way up to telling others," Walker said.

"And the notion of coming out is different for everyone," Reid piped up. "Even once you've told most of your family and friends, assuming you choose to, there will always be situations where you're put in the position of deciding to *come out* or not."

"What do you mean?" Zeke cocked his head.

"Someone asks if your wife or girlfriend will be joining you, and you have to decide how to answer. It's assumed your partner is your brother or best friend, do you correct the assumption or let it go? A distasteful joke is made about a faggot or fairy, do you laugh it off or speak up?" Reid shrugged. "It's ongoing."

"Gee, that's inspirational." Zeke frowned and rubbed the back of his neck. "Thanks."

"Baby steps. No need to deal with everything all at once," Walker assured Zeke and elbowed Reid.

The men spent the rest of the night looking up bars

and nightclubs and making plans to visit them over the next few weeks. By the time Reid and Walker left, Zeke was ready for bed and promised to bring the dogs back to the main house in the morning.

"Thanks for trusting us enough to come out to us," Reid gave Zeke a hug. "We're here, always. You're not alone."

"Thanks," Zeke whispered.

They heard the door lock behind them as they headed home.

"Wow, that was quite the night, huh?" Walker whistled.

"Definitely," Reid agreed. "I feel honored he told us. Makes me feel that our love for each other helped him in some way."

"Yeah, that's a nice way to look at it." Walker squeezed Reid's hand. "It's not going to be easy. He'll have his ups and downs. This isn't the greatest area to be a baby gay."

"But he's got us with him and on his side. We'll help him through it," Reid insisted.

"True," Walker agreed.

"I want to go check on Buttercup and Cinnamon, okay?" Reid headed toward the barn.

"It's late," Walker whined.

"Go on in." Reid waved toward the house. "I'll be there in a second. I just want to say hi to them and make sure they're tucked in tight."

"I'm sure the guys took care of them, but whatever." Walker chuckled. "Look at you all gaga over your horse babies."

Reid rolled his eyes. "You'll need the time I'm gone to wash off all that makeup. Elise has a heavy hand."

Walker pulled Reid close and rocked their hips together. "Mmmm, you can leave your makeup on if you want. Makes you look all kinds of sexy."

"Noted. Who knew you were into the femme look," Reid teased.

"I'm into whatever look *you* want to wear. Masculine, feminine, and anything in between. You know why?" Walker gripped Reid's ass and nibbled at his jawline.

"Why?" Reid breathed and threw his head back so Walker could kiss his neck.

"Because I." Kiss. "Love." Kiss. "You." Kiss. "For." Kiss. "You." Kiss. "Period." Kiss. "Always." Kiss.

"Mmmm, I like that answer," Reid moaned. "Go shower. I'll be right behind you."

Reid turned to the barn and yelped when Walker smacked his ass.

"Hurry up," Walker demanded. "I have every intention of *being right behind you.*"

Reid's laughter could be heard as he neared the barn.

Walker shook his head and climbed the steps to the house.

"Put your legs around my waist and hold on tight," Walker commanded as he lifted Reid off his feet and pressed his back against the shower wall. "I want to remember this moment forever," Walker growled as his rock-hard cock pressed into Reid's body.

Reid moaned as he sank onto Walker's steely length. "Why?" he gasped.

"Because you're absolutely fucking perfectly gorgeous with your makeup running, mascara rings under your eyes, your hair wet and messy, and that perfect mouth," Walker kissed him, "making those breathy little sounds as my cock owns your ass."

"Take me to bed," Reid demanded. "I want to be pinned under you."

Rinsing quickly and grabbing towels, the two all but ran to the bed.

"Lay flat on your stomach," Walker commanded. He slicked his finger and pressed it between the fleshy globes of Reid's ass to tease at Reid's hole.

"I'm stretched, damn it. I was just impaled on your cock," Reid panted, "get back inside me."

Walker pushed his cock between Reid's cheeks and slid easily into Reid's waiting hole. Stretching his body over Reid's, Walker pumped slowly in and out while snaking his arms under Reid's chest and holding him tight and close. "Damn, you're beyond tight this way,"

Walker grunted. Within moments, his larger body tensed on top of Reid's and he groaned his release.

"Fuck, baby, I'm sorry," Walker grumbled as he rested on Reid's back. "I didn't mean to get off before you."

"It's okay. That was good, I loved being trapped under you like that," Reid mumbled. "Having you lose control was hot."

Walker pulled from Reid's body slowly. "Roll over," he demanded.

"Seriously, I'm good," Reid tried to argue, but he was rolled to his back and his aching cock sucked into Walker's mouth. "Oh God, that's so fucking good," Reid whispered.

Walker swallowed Reid's length while fingering Reid's used hole. "Come for me, baby," Walker demanded. "I want to taste you on my tongue, in my throat." He inserted another finger into Reid's ass.

Reid's body tightened, his balls drew up, and his ass clenched around Walker's fingers while he pumped himself into Walker's greedy mouth.

Once they'd cleaned up, Walker pulled Reid close and covered them with the quilt. "I love you," he whispered as he kissed Reid's head.

"I love you, too, cowboy," Reid replied and snuggled into Walker's arms.

∾

THE MEN HAD BEEN asleep for barely an hour when they were jerked awake by Norma bursting through the door to Walker's room.

"The barn's on fire!" Norma yelled before running from the room.

Reid and Walker launched themselves from bed and threw on pants while grabbing shirts and running from the room. Shoving their feet into boots at the door, they ran toward the barn within two minutes of Norma's arrival.

"The animals are all out," Norma hollered. "Get buckets and soak the exterior. We've got the hose spraying on the hay and flammable items in here."

By the time the volunteer fire department arrived with the police hot on their heels, the barn fire was completely out thanks to teamwork and precision on the part of the ranch employees.

Thirty minutes later, Reid and Walker sat at the kitchen table with Norma and Officer Toweler. The ragged group rubbed at stinging eyes and cleared their burning throats.

Toweler flipped through his notes as Norma refilled coffee cups. "I just want to go through these notes once more to make sure I've got everything." The officer took a sip of coffee. "Reid and Walker, you were with Zeke babysitting Elise until late."

The two men nodded wearily.

"Norma, you fell asleep on the couch and woke

when one of the hands banged on the door yelling about the fire?"

"Yes, sir," Norma stated. "Dusty was on a late-night patrol and smelled smoke. Said he went to check the animals and the smoke was stronger. When he walked into the barn, he saw the hay bales were smoldering."

"From what the firemen can tell, a couple bales burned fairly quickly, but the fire slowed down when it hit some green hay." Toweler scribbled on the page as he spoke.

"Damn good luck those new bales were put up too soon," Walker mumbled.

"You two notice anything when you walked back from Wes's?" Officer Toweler asked.

"No," Reid shook his head. "I checked on the horses, and there wasn't anything out of place or different. The animals would have been stirred up if someone was in the barn."

"How long were you in the barn?" Toweler asked.

Reid frowned. "Fifteen minutes?"

"And you went straight to the house after?" Officer Toweler continued.

"I was still in the shower when he came in," Walker interrupted, "so he couldn't have been gone much longer than ten to fifteen minutes. And I really don't like where it feels like you're going with these questions."

Mark Toweler sighed and pinched the bridge of his nose. "Not where I want to go with the questions either, but Reid was the last one in the barn before the fire. It makes sense that he'd be questioned."

Reid gaped. "Wait, you think *I* set the fire?"

"No," Walker gritted out. "*I* don't."

"But you do?" Reid asked Mark.

"Honestly?" Toweler hedged. "No, I don't think you set the fire. I think you were in the wrong place at the wrong time and someone lucked out with making you look like the suspect."

"I didn't set the fire," Reid sputtered. "I'd never hurt the animals or the ranch like that."

"It's not even a question," Walker growled. "No one thinks you set the fire."

"Oh my God," Reid groaned. "The whole ranch is going to think I did it."

"Horseshit," Walker exploded. "Not a single person on this ranch would ever believe you'd set a fire."

"The one thing you've got going for you is that the timeline doesn't match." Toweler flipped through pages in his notebook again. "If you had started the fire, the damp bales would have burned more. Fire might have gotten to more dry tinder." Toweler made a note. "The fire was likely started after you left the barn, but probably not long after."

Reid lay his head on the table.

He was still sitting with his head buried when Walker came back to the kitchen after seeing Officer Toweler out.

"You know it wasn't me," Reid cried. "Please tell me you know it wasn't me."

"Stop." Walker gripped Reid's shoulder.

"I know it was my dad, or whatever loser he has working for him," Reid grumbled. "Maybe I was wrong."

"Wrong?" Walker pulled out a chair and sat beside Reid.

"Maybe it would be best to take the deal Jack offered." Reid shivered. "He promised to help you find a new ranch. We'd have the money from the sale and then half of what he sells it for. We'd be set."

"What the hell?" Walker grabbed Reid's knee and turned him. "Please tell me you're bullshitting me. What the damn hell? How would that help anything?"

Reid sighed. "He's never going to stop. The dead cows, the poisoning, the fire, it will just continue until he gets what he wants."

"He will get careless."

"Jack Alexander doesn't do careless," Reid snorted.

"Then he'll get too sure of himself and make a mistake. Or one of his lackeys will screw up. Jack is too narcissistic, and he will say the wrong thing to the wrong person. He won't be able to keep his mouth shut." Walker squeezed Reid's knee. "We *will* get him. This *will* stop. Don't you *ever* think about letting him win. Even if you and I were to be set with a job and money, think about the rest of the people here. Good, hardworking people would be left with nothing."

Reid took a deep breath. "I know you're right, I do. But I'm so tired of everything, the threats and danger, the never knowing what's next. Maybe in the long run we'd do them all a favor if we sell."

Walker's nostrils flared. "Is that what you want?"

Reid turned red-rimmed eyes toward Walker and shook his head. "No, not at all."

"Then shut it with the giving up and selling," Walker's words were gruff. "We'll get through this. Together. You and me. And everyone on the ranch. Jack Alexander won't win."

"Well, at least not *that* Jack Alexander," Reid muttered. "But I'm hoping *Grandpa* Jack Alexander wins in the end."

"I hope Grandpa Jack wipes the damn floor with Jack Junior," Walker added. "Now, come on, we need to go to bed. We're going to be dead tired tomorrow."

"I think a nap should be scheduled into our day," Reid murmured as he stood and curled under Walker's arm as they walked from the kitchen.

"I think that can be arranged."

## 19

"Don't let on that this has any alcohol in it," the guy Zeke had just met said as he sat a glass in front of Zeke. "I'd prefer not to get in trouble for contributing to the delinquency of a minor."

*What the fuck am I doing? I accept that I'm gay and next thing I know I'm meeting some dude from a dating app without letting a single person know where I'm at. At least it's a public place. Yeah, in the next town over, idiot.*

Zeke smiled at Pat and fidgeted with the napkin as he sipped the drink.

*He's cute. Would this be considered a date? Oh my God, Walker and Reid are gonna kill me.*

Zeke realized Pat had asked him a question and was awaiting his answer. "Oh, um, sorry." Zeke grimaced.

"It's okay," Pat assured. "You nervous?"

"Little bit, yeah," Zeke replied.

"So, you said you work on a ranch, right?" Pat sipped his drink and directed the conversation.

Zeke took the lifeline. "Yeah, my sister and her husband moved there. I moved with them. Didn't plan to stick around, but I've gotten pretty used to it. Still don't know if I'll stay, but for now, it's not too bad."

"What do you do? Milk cows or something?" Pat swirled his drink.

Zeke laughed. "No, we're a horse ranch. We've got some cattle, mostly beef, a few dairy. I work with the horses, mend fences, bale hay, stock the feed, that type of stuff." He finished off his drink.

"Want another?" Pat asked.

"Nah, better not press my underage luck," Zeke teased.

"Okay, mind if I get one?" Pat shook his glass.

"No, that's fine. I'm gonna run to the restroom." Zeke stood.

A few minutes later, Zeke headed back toward the table, but a loud conversation caught his attention.

"That ranch is going to be mine," a well-polished man in a suit spoke in a smooth voice as he sipped a dark amber liquid.

Zeke ducked behind a plant and pretended to tie his shoe.

"Look, I've done every single thing you've asked and they don't seem to be budging," the man's companion whined. "I don't know how much longer I can do your bidding. One of my guys is already sitting in jail because of his part in your schemes."

"I'm paying you very well to do as I ask." Zeke noticed Mr. Suit's voice took on a threatening quality. "I pay you, you find people to do the job. I'm not asking you to judge the timeline. My son may be stubborn, but I'll eventually smoke them out."

"Smoke them out," Mr. Henchman barked. "Funny."

"That fire should have done a lot more damage," Suit accused.

"Sorry, I had to do that one myself. I don't know much about farms, I didn't realize the hay wouldn't burn well," Hench answered.

Zeke shifted to untie and tie his other shoe as he questioned his sanity over what he planned to do. He peeked around the plant.

"No matter," Suit bit out and waved off Henchy. "It was probably enough to make Reid look bad. Now we just have to up the game."

"Up the game? You've already paid us to kill cows and start fires. What else do you have in mind?"

"We're going to have to hit Reid and Walker where it hurts the most," Suit growled.

Zeke walked as if in a dream. He reached the two men at the table before he even knew exactly what he was doing.

"Are you Jack Alexander?" he asked the man in the suit.

"I am, who wants to know?" Jack sneered over his drink.

"I'm Ezekiel. I work at Pine Ridge." Zeke crossed his arms over his chest and cocked his head, waiting.

Jack's companion jerked his head in Zeke's direction, but Alexander played it cool.

"What can I do for you, son?"

"You really going to pretend that you didn't just sit here and talk about all the shit you've paid this asshole to do at the ranch?" Zeke scoffed. "Unbelievable."

Pat found him and placed a hand on his shoulder. "Zeke, you good?"

"I'm fine." Zeke nodded but never took his eyes from Jack. "This *gentleman*, and I use the term loosely, was just telling his buddy here about the cows he's killed, the guns he's fired to spook horses, and the fire he started at the ranch where I work."

"Nonsense, son, I said nothing of the sort." Jack smirked and sat back in his chair while sipping from his glass.

"Oh, my bad, those are just the things you *paid* your lacky to do," Zeke bit out.

Pat attempted to steer Zeke away. "Let's go back to the table."

"No, this asshole just admitted to trying to destroy a business and piece of land and hinted at upping the severity of what he's doing." Zeke stepped closer to the table. "I want to hear him say it."

Jack cocked his head. "Did my faggot son corrupt you? Does anyone else on the ranch know you're gay?" He eyed Pat's hand on Zeke's shoulder.

Ezekiel's nostrils flared and he shrugged Pat's hand away.

Pat grunted and walked away with a dismissive wave of his hand.

"Uh-oh, I think your boyfriend is upset," Jack taunted.

"He's not my boyfriend," Zeke gritted out.

Jack narrowed his eyes. "Here's what's going to happen. You're going to walk out of here, go home, and forget everything you *think* you heard." He sneered. "If you pursue whatever you think you've discovered, I'll have no choice but to out you to not only the ranch but the entire town."

Zeke clenched his jaw and stared at Jack for several moments while seeming to weigh his options. Without another word, Zeke turned and walked away.

"You, sir, are *not* welcome at this home," Norma snarled when she swung open the front door to find Jack Alexander a few days later.

"Good morning, ma'am." Jack tipped his ridiculous

cowboy hat before removing it and holding it against his chest. "You must be the beautiful Norma. I've heard nothing but good things about your amazing cooking. I'd love to sample it while I'm here."

"Again, *sir*, you are not welcome here." Norma stood her ground at the door.

"I'd just a like a few moments with my son, please. Could you let him know I'm here?" Jack winked.

Norma huffed and rolled her eyes. Without moving from the door, she hollered over her shoulder. "Reid! Walker! The dogs must have dragged up some vermin from the brush and left it on the porch. Needs to be disposed of pronto."

Jack had the audacity to smirk. "You're adorable."

"Shut it, Alexander," Norma bit out. "You're the worst kind of bully. You're concerned with only yourself, you're dangerous, and you don't have a caring bone in your body."

Jack glanced over Norma's shoulder. "Ah, son, good to see you."

Reid snorted. "What do you want?" he asked as he took hold of Walker's hand and jutted his chin defiantly.

"May I come in for a few moments?" Jack took a step forward.

"Go on, Norma. We'll deal with this," Walker said softly.

Norma turned a scowl toward Walker. "I'll scrounge up some coffee and pastries if you'd like," she hedged.

"You're nothing if not the ever-perfect hostess, but no thank you," Reid answered. "That won't be at all necessary."

Norma's eyes twinkled. "Very well." She nodded as she made her way toward the kitchen. "I'll look into some phone calls that need made. Exterminator on top of that list."

Reid and Walker chuckled before turning to Jack.

"Could we sit?" Jack motioned to the sitting room couch and chairs.

"No need," Reid growled. "Say whatever you have to say then leave. We're not interested, but feel free to speak your piece."

Jack clenched his jaw but simply nodded. "I want to make one final offer on that deal we discussed."

"The one where you offered to buy the ranch for more than any other buyer, sell the ranch, and give me half of what you make in that sale?" Reid crossed his arms over his chest. "That deal?"

"Yes, but don't forget also assuring Walker is placed on another ranch. However, I'd like to sweeten the deal," Jack purred.

Reid and Walker waited.

"I'd like to offer you equal shares in whatever business I set up after selling the ranch." Jack shared his addendum and smiled broadly. "I think you'll find the deal much too amazing to pass up."

Reid and Walker turned to look at each other.

"What do you think?" Reid asked.

"I think we know the answer," Walker answered.

"You're right. It's not even a discussion after that addition." Reid nodded. "You want to give the answer?"

"Do it together?" Walker suggested.

Reid shrugged.

They turned back to Jack.

"No," they stated in firm unison.

Jack threw his hat to the floor. "What the hell is wrong with the two of you? You're going to regret this. You're going to lose money, lose your jobs, lose all hope for the future."

"Tsk, tsk," Walker clicked his tongue. "So angry, so many threats. Almost makes me wonder if you're behind all the shit that's been going on here."

"He is," Zeke spoke from behind them.

Reid and Walker turned around to find Zeke, Wes, Shay, and Norma standing with their arms crossed over their chests.

"Boy, don't forget what I said, there's a lot at stake," Jack warned.

Zeke shrugged. "So, some of you already knew this, some of you didn't. But long story short, I'm gay."

Jack blanched white and imitated a fish out of water.

"I ran into Jack the other night," Zeke began.

"He was in a bar, underage drinking, with an older man," Jack sputtered.

Reid's eyes bugged.

Walker coughed.

"Okay, so I know that wasn't exactly what we discussed," Zeke continued.

"We can talk about that later," Walker answered. "Go on."

"I overhead good ol' Jack here talking to his lackey about the jobs he'd already ordered and how he's planning to up the stakes. I believe the words he used were 'smoke them out' and 'hit Reid and Walker where it hurts most.'" Zeke paused and waited.

Reid and Walker turned to wait for Jack's reply.

Jack started laughing. "So, faggot farmhand tattles on me to my faggot son. So what? Big deal. You want the truth? Fine. It will be your word against mine. Yeah, I put a few things into motion in hopes of getting you off the ranch. What are you going to do about it? I'll tell you what, absolutely nothing. If you don't take the offer on the table, I'll keep at it until you have no choice and this place will be such a wreck that it won't be salvageable let alone sellable."

"You did it? All of it? The fireworks? The gun shots? The poison? The dead cows? The fire?" Reid asked.

"Not me personally, but yes, my man did exactly what I told him to do." Jack smiled smugly. "And he'll keep it up or I'll find someone else to do it. This ranch will be mine."

"You're the most disgusting excuse for a human

being I've ever had the displeasure of meeting," Walker growled.

"That may be, but I'll win. I always do." Jack shrugged.

"What is it about this ranch that you want so badly?" Reid cocked his head.

"It's a sound business investment," Jack answered. "Buy it, let the geothermal company pay top dollar for the areas they're interested in, sell the rest. Maybe a factory? Apartments? A park? Who knows, but I'm a businessman, and I know what I'm doing."

"Bullshit," Reid spat. "There's more to it than that, but I can't for the life of me figure out what it is."

Norma stepped forward. "So, you killed animals, put people's lives in danger, and tried to burn down the entire barn all because you can't stand the thought of your son getting the land you assumed your father would leave to you?"

"Nonsense," Jack sneered. "I killed animals, put people's lives in danger, and tried to burn down the barn because I want the profits this land will eventually bring in for me. It's a long-term project."

"And you just think you'll get away with it?" Wes snarled.

"Look around. I *am* getting away with it." Jack gestured widely with his arms. "Three faggots and their fan club aren't going to stop me."

"No, but I am," Officer Toweler stepped into the

room with three officers around him, guns drawn and pointed at Jack. "Norma, thank you so much for the coffee and cake invitation this morning, mighty kind of you. Who knew we'd get such an earful of information along with our breakfast?" Toweler stepped toward Alexander while pulling handcuffs from his pocket. "Jack Alexander, you're under arrest. You have the right to remain silent..." The one-sided conversation continued as the officers led Jack out the front door and to one of the squad cars.

Six people watched with wide eyes until the officers and Jack were out of sight.

"Norma, you're a freaking genius," Reid exclaimed as he hugged the older woman.

"Well, while I'd agree with that, I did nothing but open the door to that asshole," Norma stated. "I believe Ezekiel here is our hero."

Everyone turned to gawk at Zeke.

The younger man shrugged. "I saw him pull in. After talking to him the other night, I figured having the police here wouldn't hurt. I knew Norma would be fine with guests. It worked out perfectly. He'd threatened to out me if I told you what I'd heard. But you guys getting him to state so clearly all that he'd done was amazing."

"And we didn't even know the police were in the other room," Reid whooped.

"Sorry you had to find out I'm gay this way," Zeke whispered to Shay and Wes.

"We love you no matter what, always," Shay answered and pulled him into a hug.

"I'm *not* okay with you going to a bar and meeting a guy," Walker scolded. "I thought we had a plan for all of that?"

"Sorry, it was sort of spur of the moment." Zeke ducked his head. "And it ended up working out for the best."

"Did you like the guy you met?" Reid asked.

Zeke blushed. "Eh, he was okay. He left when I wouldn't stop questioning Jack and come back to the table."

"Not worth your time then," Reid declared.

"This time may have worked out," Walker continued, "but next time, we go out scouting together. And you let us vet the guys you're talking to on dating apps. At least for a while."

"You're a baby gay. You can't just jump right in with no support," Reid stated. "You need the guidance of your Godas."

"Godas?" Walker frowned.

"Gay Yodas," Reid quipped. "That's us," he whispered theatrically.

Walker pinched the bridge of his nose.

Zeke snorted.

Wes, Shay, and Norma laughed.

"Yeah, I got it." Walker pulled Reid close to his side and kissed the top of his head.

Wes cleared his throat. "So, does this mean the ranch is safe? Our jobs are safe?"

Walker nodded. "As far as I'm concerned, yes."

"And look at you," Norma patted Reid's cheek. "The man who hated horses and was leaving as soon as possible, we've turned you into a cowboy after all."

"He's the most reluctant cowboy I've ever seen," Walker teased, "but he's all mine."

They all laughed.

"All right, enough," Reid declared with mock sternness. "We've got a ranch to run. After all, a ranch is only as good as those in charge lead it to be." Reid winked at Walker. "Let's get to work."

## EPILOGUE

*O*ne *year later.*

"Those two are like a couple little old...," Reid started, "oh wait, they *are* little old ladies." He chuckled.

"Shut it, child," Norma snapped good-naturedly. "I've been lonely on this ranch for too long. Having Rachel here is a dream come true."

"You two giggle and gossip and scheme for hours at a time," Walker stated. "Grandma, you've been here almost a year, how can you ladies have *that* much to talk about every day?"

"We have a lot of time to catch up on." Rachel shrugged. "You and Reid never seem to have trouble coming up with things to talk about," she pointed out.

"Well, we're not always just talking," Reid teased.

"Speaking of grandbabies," Norma began.

"We were speaking of no such thing," Walker groused.

"We are now," Norma continued.

"Need I remind you that ass babies are only in fictional stories." Reid cocked his head. "Yes, I know you've both been reading male pregnancy romance novels."

"I believe that's referred to as 'MPreg,'" Walker chuckled. "You two know that Reid and I want children, but we can't just pop them out like some other couples. It takes planning. Do we want a surrogate? Adoption? Fostering? There's a lot to consider."

"And while we know you two are ready to board the Grandma Train," Reid began.

"Choo-choo!" Norma and Rachel interrupted and fell into each other laughing.

"*We* would like a little more time with just the two of us before we become fathers," Reid finished with a chuckle and roll of his eyes.

A knock sounded at the door.

"Come in," Walker hollered.

Zeke and the newest ranch hire, Jordan, entered the ranch house. Jordan's arrival at the ranch six months earlier had brightened Zeke's demeanor exponentially. While the two hadn't been seen together romantically or made any type of official announcement, Zeke and Jordan were basically inseparable.

Reid beamed at their arrival. "Well, if it isn't my

favorite little duo," he teased and both Zeke and Jordan rolled their eyes while blushing.

"Did you guys hear the latest news?" Zeke asked.

"You two are madly in love and finally making it official?" Reid offered.

"Wes was in town," Zeke continued, ignoring Reid's incessant matchmaking, "he saw Toweler. I guess he'll probably give you a call or come visit, but from what Wes said, Toweler said Jack will likely stay in jail for a while. Definitely not letting him out on bail now that it's been proven he's a flight risk. How desperate and dumb was he to try to make overseas travel plans. Surely he should have known all of his contacts would be bugged or working for the police."

"Jack is enough of a narcissist that he thinks he's invincible," Reid stated with a snarl.

"I'm glad he's getting punishment for what he did here, but I think it's amazing he's also getting his due for all the other illegal shit he's pulled over the years," Walker added.

"It gets better," Zeke went on, "come to find out, there's supposedly well over a million dollars worth of gold, diamonds, stocks and bonds buried somewhere here on the ranch."

"What?" Reid choked out. "*That's* why he was so dead set on buying the ranch. He wanted to get that loot before selling it and destroying it."

"That's what Toweler said too," Zeke agreed.

"Do they have details about where this is suppos- edly buried?" Walker asked. "And if it's legit or dirty money?"

"No." Zeke shook his head. "Wes said Toweler told him they'd keep on Jack about the location and where it came from. They learned of it when Jack bragged about it to another inmate. He doesn't know they know about it. So they are going to try to get more out of him."

"I'll give Toweler a call and make sure this informa- tion doesn't get out to the general public," Walker said. "Need you all to keep it quiet, too. We don't need a bunch of thieves sneaking onto our land trying to dig up a treasure that may or may not even exist."

Everyone nodded their agreement.

"You two will stay for lunch," Norma ordered Zeke and Jordan.

The two young men simply shrugged and smiled.

"Come on, y'all, it's time to eat." Norma swept to the kitchen. "Enchiladas, rice, beans, and chocolate cake for dessert."

Everyone groaned in anticipation and gathered around the table.

"After lunch, we've got a shit ton of work to do, so eat up," Walker commanded.

Reid glanced around the ranch house table at the people who had become his true family on a piece of land he had come to love with every bone in his body.

"Whatcha thinking?" Walker leaned over and whispered in Reid's ear.

"Just that I owe Grandpa Jack the biggest fucking *thank you* in the world," Reid replied as he turned teary eyes toward Walker.

"I'm grateful for his decision every damn day," Walker agreed. "You may have come into my life angry and resentful and determined to wash your hands of this place, but the land, the animals, maybe even the spirit of Jack kept you here, and I'm so damn glad."

"Guess I really am a ranch owner, huh? A real cowboy?" Reid nudged Walker's shoulder with his own.

"Like I've said before, the most reluctant cowboy I've seen, but you're *mine* and I love you more each and every day."

"I love you, too, cowboy."

## ALSO BY A.D. ELLIS

The BJ Boys (The Blueridge Junction Boys)

Something About Him

Saving Us

# ACKNOWLEDGMENTS

This is always one of the hardest parts of finishing a book, but quite possibly the most important part! It's so hard because I fear I'll miss someone who has helped me out, supported me, been a listening ear, or offered advice and encouragement. If I miss listing your name here, please know it wasn't on purpose, and I love you dearly!

Thank you, Brett, as always. Don't ever doubt your potential and how lucky people are to know you.

And, to Gage. You are truly an amazing person. Thank you, again, for all of your help and input. Not to get all mushy, but you have an incredible future ahead of you because you can do absolutely anything you set your mind to. I feel blessed to get to watch you reach the stars.

To my dear beta readers. Your input, feedback, and encouragement has proven invaluable to me! I truly trust you all and value your opinions more than you'll probably ever understand. Thank you to my newest betas as well. When I needed fresh new eyes who had never read any of these characters you were there for me and helped me so much!

To my Ellis Elite Private Discussion Group— THANK YOU! Those of you who list me in contests and comments and shout outs all the time, you're amazing and I love you for always working to get my name out there! If I start naming people here, I'll be sure to miss some; just know if you've ever shared my name or my books, it means the world to me and I appreciate you more than you'll ever know!

To my READERS!! You are what keeps me going. You are the reason I write some days. When I don't feel like I have it in me, I'll get a message or comment from a reader about how a story of mine has touched them, and *that* will be the inspiration and motivation for me to write. As long as these stories are in my head, I'll keep sharing them with you.

To the BLOGGERS who read and review and share my books!! You are beyond a shadow of a doubt some of the most dedicated and selfless people I've ever known! Thank you so much for being such a support to those of us who have stories to tell. I love BLOGGERS!

To my Juice Box ladies! Thank you so much for welcoming me into your crew and sharing your knowledge, experience, advice, and fun with me! Having some real-life authors/friends I can collaborate with is a great feeling. Dance parties, lunches, movies, videos, wine, painting, pizza, sushi, cookies...the list goes on and on! Thank you for letting me be a Juice Boxer!

To my fellow authors. Those of you who read my work, share your work with me, cross-promote with me, and offer advice and support, THANK YOU! You make this a little easier and enjoyable.

To my family and friends. I know most of you don't understand my obsession with getting these stories out of my head and on paper, but you're proud of me either way. Some of you get to read my books, some of you get to see cover ideas, some of you have to watch me lose myself in a story, some of you have to hear me vent about the hard parts of all of this; all of you love me and support me and for that, I am truly lucky and grateful.

# ABOUT THE AUTHOR

A.D. Ellis is an Indiana girl, born and raised. She spends much of her time in central Indiana teaching alternative education in the inner city of Indianapolis, and being a mom to two amazing school-aged children. A lot of her time is also devoted to phone call avoidance and her hatred of cooking.

She loves chocolate, wine, pizza, and naps along with reading and writing romance. These loves don't leave much time for housework, much to the chagrin of her husband of nearly two decades. Who would pick cleaning the house over a nap or a good book? She uses any extra time to increase her fluency in sarcasm.

FREE books-- sign up at bit.ly/ADEllisNews for a FREE male/female romance. Sign up at http://www.subscribepage.com/ADEllisNewsMMRomance for a FREE male/male romance book.

Facebook www.facebook.com/adellisauthor

Twitter www.twitter.com/ADEllisAuthor

Website http://adellisauthor.com/